Chri

Dearest Dadd

A very Happy Christmas
to you from Auckland.

Enjoy!

With love from

Little Katie

xxx

Auckland

Our City
Series editor: Ian Watt

The *Our City* series offers a new perspective on New Zealand's major cities. Each volume presents a selection of the literature inspired by one of New Zealand's four major cities. Chosen with care by a well-known editor from each city, the selections include short stories, poems, and extracts from novels and writers' memoirs. Each contributor, whether contemporary or historical, has a strong association with the city concerned, and every selection has something significant to say about the character of the city. Together they create a vivid picture of what makes the city unique.

Auckland (ed. Witi Ihimaera)
Wellington (ed. Kate Camp)
Christchurch (ed. Anna Rogers)
Dunedin (ed. Christine Johnston)

Auckland

The city in literature

edited by

Witi Ihimaera

EXISLE
PUBLISHING

First published 2003

Exisle Publishing Limited,
P.O. Box 60-490, Titirangi, Auckland 1230.
www.exisle.co.nz

Volume copyright © Exisle Publishing 2003
Original copyright holders retain copyright of individual works (see page 235).

ISBN 0-908988-36-2

Design and production by *Book*NZ (www.booknz.co.nz)
Cover illustration by Jacqueline Henderson
Printed in China through Colorcraft Ltd., HK

CONTENTS

Introduction
Auckland: The place desired by many

The Maori name for Auckland is Tamaki makau rau, often translated as Tamaki of a hundred lovers. Tamaki was a Maori chief who lived in the early 18th century, and his pa was on One Tree Hill. But the reference to the 'hundred lovers' did not only refer to any personal vigour he might have had; it was also a reference to the place that took his name, Tamaki, and how this place, today known as Auckland, has always been desired by many.

Has it ever! From Maori times, when this isthmus built on 48 volcanoes was a crucial political hub fought over by various tribes until Ngati Whatua achieved domination, Auckland has become arguably the hub of all political, cultural and financial life in New Zealand. It's still the hub for Maori, with at least 70 percent of the population living north of the Bombay hills. It's had a long and vigorous history of Pakeha settlement dating from the 1840s, which has given Auckland a remarkable entrepreneurial personality and turned the city into the largest in the country; we're actually four cities for the price of one

(Auckland Central, North Shore City, Waitakere City and Manukau City). Not only that, but since the 1950s, Auckland has had a huge influx of Samoan, Fijian, Tongan, Tokelauan and Cook Islander populations which has made it the largest Polynesian city in the world, and certainly the most populous in the Pacific. Lately, with a fast-growing Asian presence, Auckland has become one of the great cities of the Pacific rim.

While the politics of the country might be decided in Wellington, Auckland's where the action is. The gateway for many international travellers, the City of Sails is today regarded as being one of the top ten cities in the world to live in.

And the prime minister lives in Mount Albert.

———————————————

It's this quality of eclectic, anything goes, cosmopolitan, say it as it lays, flourishing exuberance that is reflected in so many of the pieces in this anthology. And it's this same sense of daring, of personal exploration of the comedy of life – of what it's like to be born and live in Auckland – that has made the compilation of the book so much fun. So many people have come to regard Auckland as their city, and we are so fortunate to have had such writers as John Logan Campbell, Bruce Mason, Frank Sargeson,

James K. Baxter and Allen Curnow – all of whom have work in this collection – to begin writing about Auckland and Aucklanders. Campbell begins this collection with a glimpse of the Arcadian possibilities of Auckland from *Poenamo* (1881), Mason represents the North Shore at its Sunday post-war best in an extract from *The End of the Golden Weather* (1962) and Sargeson takes us to Parnell in an extract from *Memoirs of a Peon* (1965). These, our distinguished elders, wrote our landscapes into existence; they created the images of the Waitemata, of Devonport, of Parnell and, through Curnow, the ravishing visions of the wild West Coast, which established for us a way, in prose and poetry, to look at who we are and where we live. Just as you might visit the City Council offices and look at old plans of Auckland, our earliest Auckland writers similarly provide our first literary maps of the city. They are our literary birth records.

Indeed, much of the fun of compiling this collection has been in the construction of a literary map of Auckland. What kind of Auckland have our writers seen? Which of our historical events have become associated with Auckland as a city? What is our whakapapa, our genealogy? Auckland has been extremely lucky to have had established authors like Maurice Shadbolt, Janet Frame,

Maurice Gee, C.K. Stead and Albert Wendt, among others, to write so magisterially about our city. Shadbolt must be the quintessential Auckland novelist; from the very beginning of his career, with *The New Zealanders* (1959), he has been Auckland's foremost chronicler, creating the template for the historical novel that many of us since have tried to emulate without success. When you read his novels, you can smell Titirangi or the salt in the sea breeze coming off the Manukau. C.K Stead is also the iconic Auckland writer, ranging wider than Shadbolt with respect to genre. He is represented with an extract from *Talking About O'Dwyer* (1999) which, along with Maurice Gee's extract from *Going West* (1992), seem to me to be as close up and personal to the West Coast as literature can get: Henderson has never had it better. Janet Frame has an extract from her luminous biography, *An Angel at my Table* (1984), which is actually about Frank Sargeson's house, recently threatened by motorway construction. North Shore City Council, back off. Sargeson has become a sacred site and he is not to be despoiled.

Indeed, a case should be made by Aucklanders for the recognition of the contribution of our writers and artists to the mapping of the heart and intellect of our city. In London, I can remember how excited I was to see the various plaques on houses that had been lived in by Oscar Wilde or Samuel Pepys. Not that we need to go as far as the enthusiastic citizens of George Eliot's work: on a visit to her home town, I discovered they loved her so much that the local pool parlour was called the George Eliot Billiard Saloon.

The established writers consolidate the representations of Auckland, but I've left the best news till last.

There's a marvellous crop of young Auckland writers and they are bringing a new sass, post-modern stylishness and superb hip-hop crunchiness to the whole business of articulating what Auckland is like in the 21st century. For some readers, Charlotte Grimshaw's work will be a new discovery; she is represented with extracts from her up-front novel, *Provocation* (1999), and if you don't recognise yourself in her work, something's definitely wrong. Diane Brown's wicked sense of humour from *if the tongue fits* (1999) perfectly captures, in my opinion, the artifice of Auckland's corporate society; going to the Auckland City Art Gallery may never be the same again.

Paula Morris in *Queen of Beauty* (2002) and Denis Baker in *On a Distant Island* (2002) are two authors who are so new that they are able to capture Auckland and Aucklanders as if they have just snapped us on a digital camera, the photographs instant and fresh. What makes their images so telling is that, like the work of Sarah Quigley, they are all the more sharp and incisive from having been set against expatriate experiences. You are sure to enjoy Morris's wonderful descriptions of Ponsonby Road and, God help us, St Luke's shopping mall, and you'll find in Baker's walk around Tamaki Drive to Parnell an evocative rendering of the reality. Similarly, Peter Wells' long career as an auteur in film sharpens the senses to Point Chevalier, and Steve Braunias's piece on Waiheke Island is surely a superb documentation of what must be one of the greatest secrets of the city, Waiheke Island itself. All of these joys of discovery and more are in this collection. Indeed, in all this multiplicity of stories, Tamaki remains the place of a hundred lovers and Auckland the place of a hundred stories. It is still the place desired by many.

I hope you will be pleasantly surprised at how our writers manage to get it right. Love us or loathe us, you will, I hope, have fun in recognising yourself in these stories, in all our gorgeousness as well as our pettiness. No doubt, like me, you'll start avoiding some Auckland establishments; even so, I am still going to push my trolley through Foodtown and try to forget that pesky writer lurking in the fruit and vegetable section jotting my every move down for posterity on his or her notepad.

Above all, however, I hope that you join me in thanking all our writers for bringing us home to the Auckland that is in each of us.

Witi Ihimaera

'Last, loneliest, loveliest, exquisite, apart –
On us, on us the unswerving season smiles …'
Rudyard Kipling

'You know what's wrong with this city? It's too damn
complicated. Auckland was never meant to be the size it is now.
We're on a tiny part of a tiny island and we're filling it up,
packing more people in – one day it's going to crack up and
slide back into the sea.'
Chad Taylor

The Waitemata waters

JOHN LOGAN CAMPBELL

Ah! never can I forget that morning when first I gazed on the Waitemata's waters. The lovely expanse of water, with its glorious colouring, stretched away to the base of Rangitoto, whose twin peaks, cutting clearly into the deep blue sky, sloped in graceful outline to the shore a thousand feet below. Still farther distant we saw a bold round high headland, backed by a still higher hill, and far away before us a long expanse of glancing waters as far as the eye could reach. Behind us basking peacefully in the morning sun lay the little island, and the reef off which we had been bumped by Wepiha the night before. The little island we could now see in all its beauty, with its crater hill, and through the broken lip we could get a peep into the crater itself. How silent and peaceful were Waitemata's lovely sloping shores as we explored them on that now long long ago morning! As we rowed over her calm waters the sound of our oars was all that broke the stillness. No, there was something more – the voices of four cannie Scotchmen and one shrewd Yankee (the sum and substance of the first invading civilisation), loud in the praise of the glorious landscape which lay before them. On that morning the open country stretched away in vast fields of fern, and Nature reigned supreme.

From *Poenamo.*

Sonnet 3

CK STEAD

October, and the kowhais declare themselves through parks
And gardens, and along the bush road to Karekare

As if someone had called on the faithful each to light a candle
And through a darkened arena the yellow flames

In their thousands flared into life. I know the darkness
These flowers make known, a spirit like water gathered

In a cup of nasturtium leaves at morning – black water
That lines the cup with silver. Let's say it's because

One evening thirty years ago as I walked to scouts
The world unveiled itself and through me burned

An ecstasy of which each moment after of life
Harbours an echo – as these kowhais hide themselves

Till the season calls them forth. My books advise
I will know that ecstasy once more before I die.

From *Twenty Two Sonnets, Poems of a Decade.*

Conversation at Karekare

PAULA MORRIS

The drive to Karekare seemed much shorter these days, Kim thought. It used to feel such a long way away, such a steep climb past the bushy verges and ski-slope driveways of Titirangi on the West Coast Road. And then that slow spiral down to the beach, twisting along a road only really wide enough for one car, stones rattling the undercarriage and the tyres skidding a little on the loose gravel every time you put your foot on the brakes. It always felt like a real adventure. Maybe the difference nowadays was that the roads were sealed – and she did have a better, faster car. Maybe, too, she'd grown more immune to distance, the way she'd learned to tolerate labour pains and spicy curries and hotter bath water.

Maybe it had never been that far away, after all.

They hadn't gone there much when they were at school. West coast beachcombing was more for the surfie set; the ones who wore shell bracelets or sharktooth earrings (illegal at their school, as were all forms of self-expression); the ones who got suspended for smoking marijuana, and spent their weekends painting orange sunsets on the sides of a van and waxing margarine-coloured surfboards – all hopelessly unfashionable and pointless activities, to her mind, then and now. They weren't part of that set, thank God: Kim had enough regrets in life without adding Indian-print skirts and a frizzy Sharon O'Neill hairstyle to the list.

But after school, when Gin was at university and Kim was trying out various career possibilities (basically, telesales and clerical work, one depressing desk after another), Karekare was somewhere they could meet. Neutral ground. They'd roll out here in Kim's old Austin, or in whatever boring piece of crap Richard was chugging around in at the time. Part of the beach's attraction was that it was absolutely free; there was nowhere to spend money, not even a dairy, and there weren't any waterfront mansions with tinted windows to remind you of what you weren't, what you didn't have. You just parked on the grass, waded across the river and trudged alongside a sand dune towards the tumbling, distant, silver-grey water.

Somewhere bigger than both of them, she supposed. Somewhere bare and empty and stern. Kim always thought of

Karekare that way; as a bad-tempered old man who didn't want you to feel at home. The black sand burned the soles of your feet and whipped across your face whenever the wind picked up, and there was no shade to speak of, unless you crossed the river again and wedged yourself against the rocks of the cliff. The lifesaving patrol's red and yellow flags never stood more than a few feet apart, swimming permitted only in the slightest sliver of sea, so even on a beach as wide and grand as this one, everyone had to splash around together like small children in a paddling pool. She hardly ever went in, anyway; you could get bowled over by a great wall of water the second you were knee-deep.

Gin enjoyed it more, and, in the old days, when Gin went swimming and Kim lay on the beach making sure the towels didn't blow away, she'd formulate theories about why that was the case – why she, spontaneous and daring, would prefer to sit still, looking at the sea, while Gin, cautious and quiet, would be out there throwing herself into giant concrete waves without a second's thought. Something to do with the artist's eye, she'd decided. And really, there was nothing more passive than engaging with a sea like this one, where swimming wasn't possible; you were a wicket, not a batsman, just knocked over and put back up again.

Kim had never been one for sport.

Her boys liked it out here. The empty vastness of it appealed to something primal in their savage little natures. They liked everything about it, except for the car ride; both were prone to sickness and evil rages when trapped in their seats for too long. But once they were set loose in the car park, there were no complaints. She'd gingerly pick her way down the short stony path to the river (weighted down with cavernous bag, chilly bin, towels, buckets and spades) and they'd be speeding ahead, looking for the deepest, murkiest place to cross. And though they weren't allowed in the sea at all, there was plenty to keep them busy at the warm, shallow end of the river, racing across the dense iron sand, pushing and shoving and falling over, like small psychotic wind spirits.

'Look at the little buggers go,' she said, pinning down a beach towel at either end with jandals. 'What have you got there?'

Virginia held up a tartan flask.

'Coffee. I'm just trying to find the other cup.'

'Bloody hell,' said Kim. 'We're not that old, are we? Flasks and sandwiches and little deck chairs. Next we'll be going for nice long drives and pointing out lovely wisteria bushes to each other.'

'Actually, I think this *is* my grandmother's.'

'There you go.'

'You must get a complimentary flask with your first pension.'

'God help us.'

'She still doesn't like it out here, by the way,' said Virginia. 'My Nana. This morning, when I told her we were coming, she told me she prefers beaches with proper-coloured sand.'

Kim laughed, pulling her pink hibiscus sarong more tightly around her hips.

'One of the other mothers at Whit's play group was asking me why the sand out here is black,' she said. 'She's Chinese, hasn't been here long. She thought it must be polluted – you know, ruined by an oil spill. I tried to explain about volcanic activity and iron content, but I got a bit stuck and confused her even more, I think.'

'Black sand,' said Virginia, drawing her fingers through it. The sand was warm only on the surface, damp and chilly underneath. 'It's not really black, is it? Sort of charcoal and bronze and copper, really.'

'People are lazy,' said Kim. She turned her head to watch the boys slapping around like caught fish in the river's shallows. 'It's easier to say black.'

'I'm glad we came out here today,' said Virginia, leaning back against the rock.

'Better than Christmas shopping at Lynn Mall, at any rate.'

'Christmas shopping and wedding post-mortems,' said Virginia. 'My mother's on at the photographer to get the pictures before Julia gets back from her honeymoon on Monday.'

'Don't tell me anything about the wedding,' said Kim. 'I'm too bitter and twisted.'

'Don't be,' said Virginia. 'You didn't miss much.'

'Let's talk about something else, then. I suppose you've seen Dick-face. What's he driving nowadays? Some sort of pretentious urban four-wheel-drive jeep piece of crap, I bet.'

'Toyota Corolla, actually.'

'Just as I suspected,' said Kim in a deep, over-dramatic voice that always made the boys laugh. She shook out her curls; they were already gritty with sand. 'Anything to report?'

'About Richard? He hasn't changed much. He just earns more money and wears more expensive clothes.'

Kim could hear something brittle in Virginia's voice; a warning, she guessed, not to ask too many questions.

'So. This Arthur guy,' she said, smacking her lips to announce the change of subject. 'What's the deal?'

'No deal.' Virginia smiled. 'Just a friend. A good friend.'

'You're shacked up with him, right?'

'Well, no. I'm just staying with him until … I find somewhere to live.'

'I see,' said Kim. She gave another loud smack of the lips. 'So you're just using him for sex.'

'No, no, no,' Virginia protested. 'No sex, no romance. Sorry. Not yet, anyway.'

'What's holding it up?'

'Me, I think,' she said, biting her bottom lip. 'And him. We're as bad as each other.'

'Backwards in coming forwards, you mean? God, I love that saying. Where did I hear it? TV, probably.'

'It's like we're waiting,' said Virginia. 'Waiting for something to happen. Waiting for someone to say something or do something.'

'Well, he should make the first move, if that's what you mean,' said Kim, who considered herself an old hand in the matter of sexual manoeuvres.

'I don't know that he will.' Virginia sounded dispirited. 'He's quite shy and eccentric.'

'Match made in bloody heaven, then.' Kim took off her

26

sunglasses; they were green and heart-shaped, and they gave her a headache if she kept them on for too long. 'What a pair you two'll make. Perhaps you should get things started. I mean, even if you do wait for him to make the first move, you could, you know, set up the board. Put all the pieces out. Hand him the dice.'

'I'd like to bring him here,' said Virginia, faltering a little as she spoke; Kim could tell without looking up that she was blushing. 'You know, one day. I don't think he's ever been anywhere like this. He's never seen the Pacific, let alone the Tasman. And I'd like to go up to Onekawa some time too, show him what it's like. Onekawa and Errington. I haven't been in years.'

'Why wait? It's only an hour away. You could go up next week.'

'Perhaps,' said Virginia. Kim followed her gaze across the river to the tall, spiky grass of the dunes. 'I'm not sure if I'm in the right state of mind yet.'

This was typical Gin, thought Kim. Anyone else would just stick on some togs, get in a car and go to the bloody beach.

'I feel like it should mean something more to me,' Virginia was saying. 'I remember Onekawa from childhood, going there with my grandparents mainly, but it's not like here. And that doesn't seem right.'

'Why not? We've been here loads, over the years.'

'But here we're day-trippers, just visiting for an hour or two. Up north it's different. It's where I'm supposed to be from.'

'Ah, I see. Roots. I don't have roots,' said Kim, though she knew she must have, somewhere – the gold fields of Otago, she'd like to think, or maybe some picturesque Yorkshire dale. Her family weren't the kind to talk about heritage and homelands; they were more preoccupied with football, tea, television. Virginia was lucky, or maybe it wasn't a question of luck at all: you got the history you deserved. Kim wouldn't have wanted a place in that elaborate line-up, all those aunties and uncles and cousins, all those stories about farms and beaches and voyages and secret deals. It was right for Gin, though. Gave her something to torture herself about as she got older, something to investigate and analyse – she was an historian, after all.

'So I'd like to go up there,' Virginia was saying, 'but only when the time's right. When I know what to look for, I suppose.'

'Go live up there, on the beach,' Kim suggested, but Virginia shrugged. 'Why not? Do what you people always did. Commune with nature, live off the land, dive for shellfish. Weave things. Grow things. Kill things.'

'Lovely.'

'You could just go for walks on the beach, you know. But you better hurry. Big developments going on up there. They say it's going to be the next Orewa.'

'It's hard to imagine.'

'Well,' said Kim. 'Not everything stays the same. I know *I'm* as youthful and glamorous as ever, but things change. Look at bloody Karekare. I mean, who are all these bastards? What are they doing on our beach?' She shook a hand towards the dozen other people on the beach. 'Haven't they got jobs to go to?'

'Maybe they're all artists,' said Virginia, lolling back on her towel, fixing Kim with a saucy stare. 'Living off the government benefit for single mothers.'

'Shut up,' said Kim. 'But speaking of motherhood, what's the time? I better reel those two in.' She stood up and waved at them, great sweeping signals. She cupped her hands around her mouth. 'Huck! Whit! Come and get some lunch. Now!'

Huck, Whit – usually she avoided running their names together like that. More than one stupid person had taken a great deal of pleasure in pointing out the implications. Ha bloody ha.

Not Virginia, of course. She would never say anything annoying and childish like that. Virginia was a true friend, the sort of person you'd always want to see again, however much time had passed. There'd always be something to say. The stuff they couldn't talk about: well, that was over and done with. There'd be things in the past they'd remember and things they'd forget: wasn't that what growing up was all about?

Kim sat back down again and reached into the chilly bin for a bottle of lemon squash. Virginia beckoned the boys in with a bag of potato chips: she was laughing at the way they were galloping, their hands curled like kangaroo's front paws.

'Look, Mummy. Sea horses!' shouted Whit, recovering from a slight stumble. Huck ran into Kim's legs and tried to bow. His head almost reached his round sandy belly. Virginia applauded.

'It's so nice to see you, Gin,' said Kim, flashing her a smile across the white cavern of chilly bin.

Virginia grinned back. 'Hey, I've got one wedding story you'll enjoy,' she said. 'I got slagged off in the toilets by the other two bridesmaids and my evil stepmother gave them a telling-off.'

'Excellent,' said Kim.

She opened her legs so Huck could sit between them on the towel.

She was glad they'd come out here today with Virginia. It wasn't hard to be friends out here, however different their real lives had become. Everything today was just as it should be: the picnic, the rocks, the river, the stories. The boys exactly at this size and this stage, still cute, still crazy. They probably wouldn't remember this particular day, but she always would. Out at the beach one more time with her friend Virginia, Karekare black and fierce and radiant all around them, the wind dropping behind the rocks, and that terrifying tide, simmering now, growing softer, almost ready to turn.

From *Queen of Beauty*.

Tamaki of a hundred lovers

MERIMERI PENFOLD

Placed in the west, Manukau spreads out.
Placed in the east, Waitemata stretches out.
Between there rises Tamaki-makau-rau,
Greenstone pendant of the ages, the beloved passed down
From Rangi standing above, Papanuku lying here!

Tamaki shifts, Makau-rau changes!
The beloved of time and the sounding tides,
'Temata at the rising sun, Manukau at the setting sun,
Lying there, lying long, hauled up by time
When night was parted from day, day, the new day!

Silent beloved of the ages, turn and see!
Here are the homes of speech: Maungawhau, Maungarei,
Maungakiekie, Rangitoto, grasped by many,
Contested by multitudes – battles fought,
And battles lost! Oh what terror!

Strangers, come, settle like godwits
On the landing-place! It is Tamaki-makau-rau!
They land at Waitemata, climb Maungawhau,
They alight at Manukau, mount Maungarei!
The forest of Tane falls, the marae of the new men lie here!

Translated by Margaret Orbell.

A view across the city

MAURICE GEE

He drives to the top of Mt Eden.

So here he is standing on a hill. If he can't make it to Duppa the crater in this one will do. Half a million people all about but here is a place where he can lie alone and see a fringe of trees and the sky – and perhaps, as he fades, a city face that looks down and does not get involved.

There are Japanese tourists in the crater. They slide on the grass as they scramble out, shrieking like birds. He approves of them; of their unbreakable foreignness. It gives him a stance to take, on top of his own hill. They pass, they click their cameras, they get in their bus and drive away; and here Jack Skeat stands, where he belongs.

The other cones rise to shoulder height: Mt Wellington, Mt Albert, One Tree Hill. Several smaller ones come up to his waist. Over the water North Head and Mt Victoria squat back to back and Rangitoto, silver-grey, rises from its glittering moat.

Crenellated, Jack thinks; but the word comes out of other histories. The shape of Rangitoto, anyway, is so familiar that he has no need for adjectives. Let it be. And while you're about it, get rid of moat.

Harry is over there, under the eye set in her ceiling, working in her two dimensional world. Harry is set at an angle. She'll come out, they will stand face to face, but not today. He lets her go and turns to the west. Another harbour glitters, five miles from the one at his back. Mud and mangrove creeks reach into the city from two sides. It would be easy to make them meet. Then ships could steam through Panmure and Otahuhu and two hundred miles would be saved.

Jack moves his finger. It is done. The Pacific Ocean meets the Tasman Sea. He is impressed. Only a true Aucklander can do that.

From *Going West*.

From the summit of Mount Eden

DENIS BAKER

From the summit of Mt Eden, looking away from the city, I could see the house I'd rented. It was an uncharacteristically warm evening for the time of year and I wasn't alone in thinking that sunset from the top of the mountain might be a nice idea. I had walked up through the paddocks to avoid the cars and buses of the winding summit road and had instead found myself disturbing a number of picnicking couples searching for a moment's solitude in the middle of the city. They all possessed the standard blanket, bottle of wine and bodily proximity and each time I saw them I tried to give them the privacy they desired. Mostly they ignored me, but one couple stared as if I was invading on this public piece of land, and I couldn't help but think they weren't going to last long if I was the most interesting thing in their evening together.

At the summit too, lovers were on the loose, arms draped around each other, but to offset them there was also a busload of

Asian tourists, and an old car with four young black-sweatered hoons. The youths were smoking up a storm, convinced of their anonymity behind windows wound tight, yet despite their efforts, the sweet smell of marijuana and the thudding of their radio drifted across the scattered crowd, turning knowing noses and lending the proceedings a music festival atmosphere.

Mt Eden was a new discovery for me. I'd grown up in a different part of the city and standing there I wondered why it had taken me so long to find it. How could I have been so regionalised as a twenty-year-old? In the few times I'd walked up here since moving into the area I'd already grown attached to the view, although I was still struggling to comprehend the way the city had grown and changed in my absence, new towers and office blocks going up everywhere. In many respects it was unrecognisable as the place I knew as a kid, the one I'd carried in my mind those ten years overseas, and it only added to the feeling of being stranded that had been growing since I'd arrived; a stranger in the place that should have been home.

'Paul, there are cows.'

'Yes.'

'In the middle of the city.'

'Ah-huh.'

Mt Eden was close with plenty of room to talk so I'd directed us that way, this time following the road to the summit instead of cutting across the grass. Still on a lower part of the mountain we were faced with a herd of cattle. They were spread across the asphalt and on the pasture verge either side. A couple of cars were waiting patiently, inching forward trying not to scare them, hoping to force them apart. The cows were unwilling to move.

'Oh my God,' she said.

Without my fully realising it, Mt Eden had become one of my favourite places in the city, partly because of the view, partly because of this rurality. Larry's words were still bouncing around my head and if I was to submit myself to this with Angela it should at least be somewhere I felt comfortable.

'It's crazy, isn't it? But it's not like they're wandering the actual streets or anything. They're well contained up here and they're only around to keep the grass down and the tourists amused.'

I watched her face and led us around them, their doleful eyes following us past. For someone so well educated, Angela had a remarkably fixed schema of how life should be. Rather than developing it over time based on her reading and limited travel experience, it had seemed to emerge from her innately and now her world operated strictly within its parameters, at times shocking her when other worlds did not coincide with hers. Not a liberal in the popular sense of the word, she was prone to intolerance of anything that didn't fit into this schema, dismissing even the most trivial differences, cultural or otherwise, as ridiculous and ignorant. Sometimes I doubted whether she truly believed in this approach, carrying it off as a way to mark her difference, but on this occasion the incredulity and disdainful looks were real. As far as she was concerned, in purportedly civilised cities like Auckland, cattle in a public park that was not entirely unlike Primrose Hill didn't fit, and I could hear her, half-cut back at a London dinner party, reporting, 'They have animals loose all over the streets.'

One of the drivers got out of his car and started herding the cattle off the road.

'It's so third world,' she said.

Two extracts from *On a Distant Island.*

Morning Maungawhau

ALBERT WENDT

Right forefinger into cord ring, pull down, that's it, release the shade, rat-ta-tat-tat-rat as it rolls up to the top of the bathroom window. Immediately, Michael is bathed in white sunshine. The window is like a live TV screen illuminating every pore of him as he stands at the sink, dressed only in his pyjama shorts, gazing up over the hedge, which he'd helped his father plant three years before, and over the roofs of the neighbouring houses at Maungawhau now drenched with egg-yellow light. Not Mt Eden, his father whispers. Mau-nga-whau. Say it. Mau-nga-whau. Michael mouths it, spelling each letter in his throat. The shadows of large clouds clamber up and over the mountains. 7.30 am. Faint smell of piss, mildew and wet towels. He reaches up, undoes the latch and pushes the window out. The crisp morning air wraps its arms around his chest, while he continues gazing up at the mountain.

Whenever his father was home – and it was now nine

months, two weeks and three days since his last visit – Michael observed and learned his father's routines and the tunes he whistled as part of those. Each day it started at 6.30 am when his father woke and went to the bathroom for what he referred to, jokingly, as his 'ablutions'. Michael would sit on the edge of the bathtub and watch.

Michael pulls his toothbrush out of the holder on the wall, puts mint Dickens, his favourite toothpaste, on it, cups a handful of water to his mouth and starts brushing. Just like he's seen his father doing so often.

As he brushes, with the icy mint tingling on his tongue, he whistles, in his head, his father's toothbrushing song:

Maungawhau, listen to my song.
Maungawhau, listen to my song.
What do you think of a man
who's never known the blues? ...

He once again *feels* his father's first whistling in his left ear. Warm and ticklish lips and breath. The first real memory of his father: that long quivering note whistled breathlessly into his ear and down into his depths until he *was* that eternal sound. When he grew to know other sounds, that one extended note reminded him of a train whistle, far away, in the night, a long drawn-out breath being sucked back by an unknown destination. That was also the theme he identified with certain people, creatures, places and situations. For instance, whenever he heard and saw whales on TV that was the sound which gripped him. When he was sad – and he tried not to be, ever – his father's first whistle embraced him. Every time he and his mother visited Uncle David at the hospital – Uncle David had been sick for years of an ailment his mother avoided naming for him – and he watched his emaciated uncle's slow breathing, while his mother talked and talked, his father's note was acutely long in his hearing, quivering like the tail of the angry scorpion he'd seen in a James Bond movie. On still, rainless evenings, Maungawhau whistled that note over their city of black glass too. So did lions in the zoo. So did the live mussels which his father loved eating raw in drawn-out slurps. So did abandoned buildings and bikes and boats; and the dirty, scrawny, derelict alkies who congregated every evening in their church hall for hot soups and bread and a bed for the night. So did Mt Eden Reordinarination Centre not far from their home. One night on their way home from the movies, and he was sitting between his parents as they drove past the prison, his mother said, 'It must be awful in there.' The grey stone walls glistened, like Darth Vader's mask, in the harsh glare of the security lights. He waited for his father to comment. His father stared ahead. When Michael glanced at the high-security centre, it sang that first note his father had breathed into his head.

> *... Maungawhau, I've known you all my life*
> *but you don't care what happens to me.*
> *Maungawhau, did you know*
> *Crumpy now sells Toyota pick-ups? ...*

His father returned to them once a year, as far back as that first whistled note. As Michael had grown up, his father's absences had lengthened into that theme too ...

Michael drops his toothbrush into the hole in the plastic holder. Looks up again at Maungawhau as he washes his hands. His father's eight-second ablution tune, a happier lilting, starts:

> *Baby, baby, don'ya luv me?*
> *Baby, baby, yar drive me crazy.*
> *Baby, baby, yar drive me crazy ...*

43

He splashes large handfuls of cold water against his face. (Just like his dad.) Some of the water splatters onto the floor. He dries his face with fierce wipes of the towel. Then, holding the bathmat under the toes of his right foot, he dries the floor with round looping movements of his leg. Again imitating his father.

He opens the medicine cabinet. His father's silver razor, in the glass in the cabinet, looks so lonely. He takes it out, takes the blade out of it, tightens it again, and, imagining a rich lather on his face, starts shaving. Looking into the mirror. And whistling:

> ... *Baby, baby, Ah luv yar true.*
> *Baby, baby, why can't yar be true?*
> *My heart aches and aches for you ...*

Every time the blade is leaden with cream, he washes it under the tap.

He glances up at the mountain. The paddocks, terraces and trees are now a darker green. Around the apex on the summit move groups of tourists, stick figures at that distance. About once a month he walked his mother up through the paddocks and scatter of cowshit (which ponged) to the summit. He hated doing it but his mother needed the exercise. They had to rest every hundred yards or so because she was so unfit. And three times out of every four climbs, they found busloads of Japanese tourists at the summit. He liked them because they seemed so together, so in a group; he liked their intense chatter and attention as they photographed the city and one another. Once, a grey-haired couple, who barely came up to his shoulder, asked his mother to take their picture with their camera. The couple stood, arms around each other, at the edge of the mouth of the dead volcano, with the immense sky and city and Waitemata Harbour and the Gulf as their backdrop. His mother took two photos. The man bowed thank you, afterwards. His wife smiled; her mouth was full of gold teeth. Another time, while his mother sat on the steps, trying to regain her breath – 'My heart, oh my heart!' she kept saying to him – he went over to the southern edge of the summit and looked down over the suburbs as they spilled away to Manukau Harbour and the white haze. As the wind cooled his sweat, he started whistling 'On Top of Old Smoky', which his father had taught him three years previously. The whole southern sprawl of the city listened, so did the orange horizon and the Waitakere Range to the southwest.

... On top of old Smoky
all covered with snow,
I lost my true lover ...

He was into the third line when he heard two whistlers beside him. Two Japanese youths, in what looked like naval uniforms, smiled at him. He nodded and whistled louder. They whistled with him. Theirs was a rich powerful chorus that burst up into the high-doming heavens. The other tourists watched. When they finished, their audience applauded. He glanced at his mother. She was on her feet, clapping too. He looked at his two friends. They bowed; he bowed back, and then hurried to his mother.

'One day, I'm going to Japan,' he said as they strolled down the mountain, on the one-way road.

'They eat strange food,' she said.

'How's your heart?'

Grinning, she put an arm round his shoulders. 'Fit and well,' she replied.

After washing his father's razor, he dries it with his towel and returns it to the glass. Then, delicately, he pats some of his father's George Eliot aftershave into his face. The bathroom is immediately alive with the scent. The neighbours are up; he can hear the couple in the back flat arguing. The sizzling of bacon being fried is loud from the front flat. They had little to do with their neighbours or anyone else who wasn't family the way his mother defined that: related by blood or loyalty, obligation and life-long friendship.

He straightens his father's gear in the medicine cabinet; cleans the sink with a wet facecloth.

… Sunday is the rest we need
after a week of sweat and misery.
Sunday's for lyin' in and waitin'
for your son to cook ya bacon and tea …

He's careful not to wake his mother as he tiptoes up the corridor past her bedroom …

Extract from 'The Don'ts of Whistling'.

Auckland, 1900

MAURICE SHADBOLT

In 1900 Auckland was home to five hundred gas lamps and fifty thousand people. A city in name if not yet in earnest, it was barely past its frontier beginnings. A canyon of robust stone buildings now hinted at permanence. Astride a lumpy isthmus, lapped by the tides of two large harbours, this unpretentious outpost of Britain remained wedded more to nature than man. ('Last, loneliest, loveliest, exquisite, apart,' romanced Rudyard Kipling on his one reconnaissance.)

The city's legal fraternity was negligible in number, parochial in outlook and clubby in character. Uncomfortable with shop talk and unpractised in gossip, Walter rubbed shoulders with few in his profession and fewer outside it. On occasion, when vocational rites demanded, Walter allowed himself to be seen in the company of colleagues at the vine-wreathed Northern Club, a stocky three-storey building in an enclave of colonial architecture just a short walk from the courts. (Globe-trotting

Anthony Trollope had stayed there and praised its surprisingly civilised amenities.) Such social occasions confirmed that Walter was an indifferent mixer; he was often seen heading for the door after one drink and two or three handshakes. On the other hand he was the kind of endearingly eccentric Victorian gentleman relatives delight in recalling. For much of the 20th century no New Zealand living room was complete without a forefather like Walter heroically attempting a smile from a silver frame on an antique sideboard. In life Walter Dove was a man who smiled sparingly and laughed reluctantly. An unhappy man? Alice never offered her thoughts on the subject; she found the question both irritating and irrelevant.

Alice met Walter when the first of her four husbands died young, leaving her with tiny twin daughters, Lucy and Jane. Her husband's confused affairs were in Walter's hands. There were unwise investments and callous creditors. Walter's distress was apparent. There were tut-tuttings and hisses of breath as he laboured through documents. 'There might,' he reported, 'be enough left to pay for the funeral.'

There wasn't. Though Alice didn't learn so till later, Walter picked up the undertaker's bill. He also arranged the sale of Alice's house and settled her in a dwelling suiting her reduced circumstances. One way and another her husband's estate was cleared of claims. Finally Walter gave her employment too.

Women were still an uncommon sight in legal offices. Responsible solely to Walter, Alice proved a competent clerk. She was also, by the measure of any era, an eye-catching one: surviving photographs show a shapely, stylish and warm-eyed girl. (Her undisguised regard for Walter made for rumour but it foundered on the fact of his rectitude.) Familiar with Walter's concerns, she could be relied on to discourage visitors when his left hand was conferring with his right. In intermittent form, these solo tête-à-têtes possibly predated Alice's appearance in the office. They became an institution, however, after her advent. At two on Friday afternoons Walter's door closed and his working week ended. He emerged from retreat three hours later, clapped his bowler hat on his head, picked up umbrella and briefcase, wished Alice a happy weekend with Lucy and Jane, and caught the 5.30 ferry across Auckland's Waitemata harbour to the marine suburb of Devonport.

From *Dove on the Waters*.

Sunday at Te Parenga

BRUCE MASON

By ten o'clock, the people of Te Parenga are abroad, liberated for a day from their caged bondage in buildings or at sinks. The beach is spattered with their clots of colour and spurting with their talk. The sea rolls on and up the sand, frothing near the grey powder by the gates and Te Parenga settles into its Sunday ravishment by sun and sea.

Promptly at eleven, Sergeant Robinson appears on the beach. He has been Te Parenga's Sergeant of Police for over thirty years. Small, fierce-eyed, round and gnarled as a nut, he strides along with a nuggety grandeur, clean white Sunday shirt blazing, no tie, helmet set just a trifle askew to show that he is not on duty, striped braces straining like hawsers over his shoulders, bowing, saluting, regally acknowledging salvoes of greetings from all over the beach.

A new fashion has recently reached Te Parenga. For the first time, men have begun to appear on the beach in shorts and are no longer encased from neck to upper thigh. This offends

51

Robbie's deeply Victorian sense of propriety. Again and again I recall scenes like this:

'Aw, gidday, Bill. Aw, not so bad. Heat gets yer. Gets all mucky, under me helmet … What's that? Gubberment? Well, whaddya expect with them jokers down a Wellington … Hey! Hey, you! And where do you think you're going. What? For a walk? Like that? All uncovered on ya top? Ya not decent! Cover yaself up, quick and lively. All a yas! Cover yaselves up!'

He lumbers off, muttering, 'Think this a nudiest colony, a somethin …'

And the men comply with towels until he has moved on, when bare flesh again emerges to peals of laughter, but not so that Robbie can hear, for he is greatly admired and respected on the beach.

'Ya gotta hand it to him, though,' is the universal tribute, 'proper ole dag …'

The golden day seeps on; no thoughts but warm, no talk but trivial until the sun fingers the eyeballs dead ahead – the sand cools, and the beach slowly empties.

On Sunday nights in the summer, we have tea on the glassed-in verandah facing Rangitoto. My mother prepares a mountain of sandwiches and out they come, mounds of them, on a jingling trolley. There we sit in the summer, while the day ends in gold explosions on the horizon and the lower borders of the sky are suddenly drenched in pink, as though a full brush had been slapped round the rim. Below us on the beach, people are strolling and the thin rarefied tinkle of their voices floats up to us as they approach, then a sudden blare of coherent sound …

'So I said to Phyllis, what's the use? Why don't you finish with him, for good and all …'

Will Phyllis give him up?

Or this, in a high, fluty voice:

'Well, I went to her house and everything on the line was silk and I thought, Mmm-mm! Mine's cotton …'

Or an urgent foreign voice:

'But Hans, why did you do it? What were you thinking of? …'

What had the man done, so far from home? … Huge questions, teasing the mind for ever. Laughter like a rocket burst, hanging on the still air in showers of sparks …

From *The End of the Golden Weather*.

Frank Sargeson's place

Janet Frame

When the summer is over, I thought, and the weather is cooler (a dream: in the cool of the evening) I shall write another novel. Emerged from my fictional world I can see clearly that my staying in the hut was using more of Frank's time, energy and feeling than he had bargained for, as I was not his only *charge* (the word in all its variety of meanings), and each (Harry, Jack, old Jim next door, Frank's two elderly aunts, one of whom was blind, who lived near the beach in an old gabled house full of high dark furniture) had to be visited and listened to and comforted, with the poorer 'charges' receiving vegetables from the garden, or a ten shilling or pound note. The visit to the aunts most consumed Frank's energy, for their tongues were sharply critical while he remained patiently docile. When he returned from seeing them, he always said, in a tone of amazement, '*My fat aunts, my huge aunts.*' And they were huge aunts with a kind of solidity that would seem to be incapable of ever melting: I think they were Frank's mother's sisters; and I think they were like the past, his past, in being unable to vanish: they were not snow-women; they were without season or time; and when the sick blind aunt lay in bed, one day when I visited with Frank, she was diminished not by her blindness or sickness but only by the tall oak bookcase that loomed by the bed.

The heat of the summer persisted. Frank began to talk of the 'golden time' in his childhood when he kept silkworms. It was a remembered summer, like 'That Summer' of his short perfect novel. It happened then that one day I was walking in Karangahape Road (a 'possession' of Auckland, like Rangitoto) when I noticed silkworms displayed in a pet-shop window. I bought half a dozen and that evening I nervously unwrapped them and set them on the kitchen counter. The sensitivity between Frank and myself was now so extreme that every movement had to be planned for fear of hurting or implying by one a state which could not be borne in the other. I had seen Frank come near to weeping over his postcards of his early European journey; I felt that the golden time of his uncle and the silkworms belonged only to him, and I did not want him to think that I, listening to his constant remembering of a childhood happiness, had dared to try to provide him with a replica of the

55

past. I was casual about the silkworms. He was delighted with an immediate, not a recollective delight. He, in his turn, viewed the silkworms as a means of absorbing *my* attention while he and I planned my next 'move' which, according to Frank, was for me to 'travel overseas' to 'broaden my experience', a convenient way, both he and I realized, of saying that I was 'better out of New Zealand before someone decided I should be in a mental hospital.' We both knew that in a conformist society there are a surprising number of 'deciders' upon the lives and fate of others. Frank even suggested that he become my next of kin in a marriage of convenience which I then found insulting, and he, on overnight reflection, decided against.

We concentrated on the silkworms, I roaming the neighbourhood of Takapuna until I found in an old-fashioned garden overlooking the beach and the pohutukawa trees, the mulberry tree with leaves to feed our 'charges', and a kindly owner willing to give me supplies of leaves. Frank brought home a shoebox from Hannahs shoe store, nestled the mulberry leaves inside and gently lay the silkworms upon the leaves. At once they began to eat. During the day we kept the box on the end of the counter near the bookcase, and at night I took it down to the hut and set it on my desk-table. We knew the silkworms were eating

56

for *dear life*. In the silence of the night as I lay in bed I heard a sound like the turning of tiny pages in a tiny library, which I've heard only since then, slightly magnified, in the library of the British Museum as the readers steadily consume page after cherished page of their chosen books. The silkworms' consuming was literal, the sound of steady chewing and chomping all night and all day, although unlistened to during the day, without pause until that stage of their life was over: a lifelong meal. Frank explained what would happen next, and we watched as the silkworms entered their next life, as they began to wave their heads in a circular motion, with a thread like the golden spiderweb being drawn from their mouths. Frank had placed each on a strip of cardboard which they used as their anchorage, enclosing themselves and the cardboard in a golden cocoon, and when all was still within, Frank gently cut through the silk, removing the naked grubs and wrapping them in nests of cottonwool – the usual intrusion based on the belief that we own the world, its creatures and its produce. The golden thread of plaited silk hung on the wall by the window in that same room where Ivan Ilych and the old Prince died, and Pierre saw Napoleon, and the oak tree budded and shed its leaves, and Mozart and Beethoven had their music played: a rich gold room.

In time, the grubs, cosy in their cottonwool, became moths which in their first moments sought each other, male and female, the males mounting the females for mating that lasted, like the eating and spinning, all day and night, until the males fell torpid, dying one by one, while the females again with their furniture provided, laid tiny rows of white eggs, like Braille dots or stitches, neatly upon the sheet of cardboard; then they also died whereupon Frank who in all the stages of the silkworms' development had repeated his actions of years ago, explaining each stage, describing how it would be, set the sheet of cardboard with the silkworms enclosed in their own past, present and future, in the shoebox, which he buried, lowering it like a makeshift coffin into the earth.

'That's the cycle,' he said, his words and his glance capturing other references, other species.

'They'll stay there the winter, and when the warm weather comes, I'll dig them up, they'll hatch, and the cycle will repeat itself.'

The completeness, perfection, and near-indestructibility of the cycle did not escape us.

That evening, like Gods, we celebrated with Vat 69 the lives dedicated to eating, spinning, mating.

The next day we planned a letter to the Literary Fund applying for a grant for me to 'travel overseas and broaden my experience.' I was now free to accept the invitation from one of Frank's friends, Paula Lincoln, known as P. T. Lincoln, or Paul, to stay at her bach at Mt Maunganui while we awaited the outcome of my application.

From *An Angel At My Table*.

Pity about the gulls

KEVIN IRELAND

Walking along the beach this morning
you could see yachts putting out
the white flags of their sails to sue

for peace on Earth, jaunty waves
leaning up against the horizon,
shelling out buckets of small change,

and an ocean liner, with a toothpaste
smile, sporting Rangitoto
on its beam like a cocked hat.

Pity about the gulls.
Heads down, backs hunched,
They humped the misery of the world,

drilling screams into the cliffs,
rubbing the shine off the day.
Always some bastard has to spoil it.

From *Selected Poems.*

View across the harbour

CHARLOTTE GRIMSHAW

Out in the harbour the yachts speed across the choppy water, the hot pink and burnt orange and yellow sails fill with hot wind, the hard light strikes the water, the sun burns down on the sunburnt, zinc-coated, sunglassed crews, the wind burns, the light is too bright, all are squinting and peering and shading their eyes against the white glare and the fierce wind and in the high, high sky not a cloud can be seen.

Under the veranda the dog lurks, seeking the deepest shade.

At the flat on the Roundabout Road Leah Levine watches the children running through a sprinkler on the lawn, the four of them screaming and gasping and falling through the spray while behind them in the house a fly screen bangs loose in the breeze and on the lawn the light makes a rainbow on the sheen of water drifting in a fine spray mist through the bright air. Bang says the screen, and the hinge wire squeaks as it flaps in the hot wind. Squeak bang. Sometimes the sky can be so blue, Leah thinks, that it is on the verge of being black. Closing her eyes she watches the photo negative of little bodies dancing and falling against the red sunrise of her lids. A fly drones around her head, darting and buzzing and spiralling down, the sheets on the line billow and flap like white flags and the fly lands, the hinge wire squeaks, the children dive and scream. Bang says the screen, smacking on the window on the sunny white wall. Squeak/squeak. Bang.

On the Lehmans' deck Carlos fills plastic containers with seashells for Millicent's garden: mussels, pipis, toheroa and scallops to cover her paths and line her borders. He has already raked over and expanded her vegetable garden, adding more plants and windbreaks and a proper little watering system with tiny jets which come up out of the ground. Such a green thumb, Millicent says, beaming through her heavy specs. The beach is dotted with groups of sunbathers lying inert on the beach towels and down at the water the swimmers splash and call as they wade out into the high tide, flapping their arms and screaming as the water chills their sensitive bits, and Carlos stops sorting shells to watch two girls fighting in the water to push each other under. They look like two Maori girls with strong brown arms and flying black hair and he thinks of his cousins long ago fighting with him in the sand around Whatuwhiwhi Beach and of his cousin May Rangi running home screaming because she had accidentally bloodied his nose and he had lain on the sand and pretended to be dead. He continues sorting shells but thinking of May Rangi, the tiny girl in her flowery tank top and shorts and the long ago upside-down view of the marram grass waving and the shiny backs of her brown legs as she raced away from him up the dune, bellowing so loudly that the adults came looking and told them off lazily – Hey you kids, behave! – and he finishes sorting the shells, puts lids on the boxes and puts them away, then sits sadly in the shade watching the beach while the sunbathers lie open-mouthed, scarlet and motionless in the coloured pools of their towels.

From *Provocation.*

A family at Devonport beach

WITI IHIMAERA

That afternoon, there is no answer when I ring the doorbell of my parents' home in Devonport. I go around the side and vault the fence to the back yard. Not even a yap from that excuse for a dog, the pampered poodle, given to my mother three years ago by my elder sister Pamela. But the ranchslider doors are wide open to the sun, the curtains billowing in the breeze from the sea.

'Is that you, David? Been waiting long?'

My father has come through the door, slipping out of his beach sandals. At seventy he is still a handsome devil, with the straight back and figure of a military man. His health and fitness are matters of pride with him. During the cold months he jogs morning and night. During summer he does a daily swim, ploughing vigorously to the wharf and back. He is the envy of men twenty years his junior.

'Dad,' I sigh, 'I've told you before about leaving the place with the doors wide open. You'll get done over one day.'

'Nonsense,' he snorts.

It's no use arguing with him. If he says something is nonsense, that is the end of the matter.

He has just come up from the beach. He wears a short robe over his swimsuit. A towel is draped over his arm. His hair is wet, slicked back. Fastidious as ever, he goes direct to the washbasket and throws the towel in.

'The children are down with your mother having a swim. Did you bring a swimsuit?'

'No.'

The beaches where I usually go are places where to wear a swimsuit is to be overdressed. Or coy. Or trespassing.

'Then take a pair of mine. In the bedroom drawer. Come to think of it, there may be a pair of yours there anyway.'

He is walking to the bathroom and doesn't see my reaction. The idea of wearing one of my father's swimsuits, pre-Speedo, does not appeal. But one of my own –

'Okay.'

From the master bedroom there is a panoramic view of this fashionable beach suburb here on the northern shore of the city. Prices for real estate have shot up since my parents first retired here seventeen years ago. Ever since, they have credited their good luck and sense.

The suburb itself is a few kilometres from the city, on the peninsula. It is an isthmus away, across the harbour bridge with its two-lane extension, dubbed the 'Nippon clip-on' because it was designed by Japanese engineers. My parents were among the first to build in what has, over the years, become progressively known by the property developers as the 'undeveloped' end of the peninsula. However, six years ago the *nouveaux riches* discovered the area and began to build palatial homes at midway or towards the boutique end, where the new tourist complex and yacht marina now stand.

The new rich have put increasing pressure on my parents and their neighbours to sell. But the older retired folk are all very happy with where they are, thank you very much. They like to think they represent a certain stability and tradition in the city. They consider themselves a bastion against the appalling consequences of the technological revolution and spread of McDonald's, Pizza Hut and other American fast-food chains. They represent good old-fashioned values in a crass world, a sense of British quality and style where the values of Commonwealth can be upheld.

The retired have structured their lives against change, against the New. Their strategies involve the time-honoured rituals of a cup of tea in bed at seven. Breakfast is at eight. One reads the morning paper until nine and does a spot of housework or tinkering with the boat. Morning tea is at ten and, after that, a visit to the library or the suburban shopping centre. One has lunch at half-past twelve, after which the men play golf or tennis and the women go to bowls. Afternoon tea is served at four. A nap might be in order, then a whisky before dinner at six. One watches the television news at seven and later the best British drama or comedy. To bed by ten with a book. Perhaps bridge on Friday. Or out on the yacht on the weekends.

Not a minute is left to chance. Every hour is accounted for. Otherwise something might get in between to disrupt, to subvert, to rock the boat.

The pathway to the beach is busy with schoolchildren rushing down for a swim. There is something about breeding and social standing which sets apart the children of the privileged. Finer boned and longer limbed, they replicate the grooming and sleek racehorse physicality of their class.

'Is that you, David?' Mrs Stockbroker and her husband, The Retired Stockbroker, are coming up the path. They live next door to my parents. 'Is Annabelle with you? No? The children are down with your mother by the Crocodile's Tail. They're simply gorgeous, my dear. Simply delightful.'

I wave in reply and hurry on down. The entire neighbourhood is besotted with the girls, who are the youngest children in the street. Already amid the shouts and yells of other older children I recognise the high, squealed commands of Rebecca and special piping sounds of Miranda. Then the beach comes into view and I see them.

The scene is pure picture postcard. Flame-petalled trees overhang the beach. Brightly coloured umbrellas spike the sand. Older children are launching their dinghies while grandparents watch. The sand is a golden dream curving around an impossibly azure sea. It is low tide and the rocks that have been dubbed the Crocodile's Tail ever since children of imagination began to swim here are exposed.

Rebecca is towing Miranda, in waterwings, toward the crocodile's jaw. Charmed, the retired on the beach watch with affection.

'I'm frightened, Becca, I'm frightened!' Miranda cries.

'Oh don't be such a wimp, Miranda,' Rebecca replies.

'But I'll drown.'

'No you won't.'

'It's such a long way to swim.'

'Don't you trust me to get us there? Just hold on tight, okay?'

When they make it, there is scattered applause from the beach. Rebecca makes a face and pulls her sister to safety.

My mother is sitting under a beach umbrella, the pampered poodle beside her, watching the girls as they clamber to the top of the Crocodile's Tail and claim it. She has sunglasses against the glare and is smoking a cigarette. She sees me approaching through the groups of sunbathers and children building sandcastles, and hastily stubs the cigarette in the sand.

'Hello, darling,' she says as I sit beside her.

She is a marvellously preserved woman who bears her years lightly. Her skin is slightly veiled with moisturiser but still has the sheen of vigour. She carries the signs of sixty-five years as does a vintage car – with grace.

Today, though, her nervousness makes her graceless.

'You don't have to hide your cigarette,' I answer.

'It's your father,' she says. 'He never likes me to smoke in the house. It's absolute agony waiting for him to go up from the beach so that I can light up.'

Her answer is evasive and she does not look at me. She takes another cigarette out of her beach bag. Her fingers shake as she lights the cigarette, inhales and breathes out the smoke.

'I know cigarettes are bad for me,' she says, 'but I just can't seem to give them up. The ones I buy have low tar, see? Are you going in? The water is lovely.'

She has not yet offered her cheek for my usual filial sign of affection. When I lean towards her she moves away.

'Go on now. Before the water gets too cold.'

My little princesses haven't noticed that I have arrived. I shall slip into the water, swim out to the open sea and sneak up on them from the other side of the Crocodile's Tail.

The water is liquid bliss. A quick duck of my head and I am totally immersed, body temperature taking on the sea's coolness. Then swift strokes seaward, careful not to be run down by the children's yachts whizzing out from the beach, around the lashing tail of the crocodile. There they are. In unguarded innocence. They have come down from the top and are entering the water again, ready for the perilous journey back to the beach.

'I can't do it, Becca!' Whimpering, Miranda slips into the sea and, straight away, begins a furious dogpaddle to the safety of the beach. 'Help me, Becca! Help me!'

Rebecca sighs and starts to push her sister, waterwings and all, through the water. 'See?' Rebecca says. 'As easy as pie.'

I go in for the attack. Underneath the water I can see pale legs just ready to be grabbed and eaten. I hold Miranda's left foot as she swims. She squeals and kicks out.

'Becca! A shark!'

'Nonsense,' Rebecca answers.

I hold one of her feet as well. Suddenly both girls are screaming for help.

'Grandma! Grandma! Save us!'

But my little princesses are too late. The Great White Pointer surfaces, has them by his teeth and is savaging them, gulp by bone-cracking gulp, tearing legs and arms from torsos, heads from bodies, oblivious of their cries of terror.

Then Rebecca says, firmly, 'That's enough, Daddy,' and the spell is broken. 'You mustn't do that to us, especially Miranda.'

Miranda is an asthmatic. Her attacks come randomly but she has an inhaler.

'Hello, Daddy,' Miranda sighs. She puts her arms around my neck, a wet bundle of curls and softness. 'It was you all along, wasn't it?'

Rebecca looks at her. 'Of course it was, silly. Anybody could see that.' Tenderly, she hugs me too.

Up on the beach my mother is shaking to pieces. She is breaking apart, her sunglasses flashing in the sun. Behind them her eyes are smoky, ablaze with fear and anger.

The girls run ahead with the pampered poodle and, by the time my mother and I arrive at the house they are already in the shower together. As usual, they argue over whether the water is too hot or too cold. When they get out my mother wraps them in towels and gives them a good rub-down. Then it's juice and biscuits, and they settle down to watch afternoon children's television.

My mother makes afternoon tea. We take it on the terrace. After idle small-talk, my father coughs and nods at me.

That is when I tell them that I have been living apart from Annabelle for some six weeks. Yes, I have taken a flat in the city. Yes, I will leave my new telephone number and am sorry that I haven't given it to them before now. No, I'm not sure if we'll get back together again. That is up to Annabelle.

My parents want to believe the best in me. They settle for the usual sympathies. These things happen. It may blow over. It will all come out in the wash. There are always occasional problems between a wife and a husband. It takes time before a marriage settles down.

Yes.

Clink of teacups.

Pity.

But it is not up to Annabelle, and because I crave my parents' respect and love, I just cannot tell them why I have left.

Oh yes, I could obscure the real facts by saying that the separation was something I had to do. I could say something to the effect that I had to work things out. Or that I had to find out who I was and what I wanted out of life. I could hide behind polite language.

But I would bring my parents' world crashing down around their ears, harbour bridge, suburbia, Uncle Tom Cobbleigh and all.

Behind the small-talk, fear.

From *Nights in the Gardens of Spain.*

Container terminal

BOB ORR

The sun rising
above Rangitoto …
there were tracks
across the tide
I stood in sunlight
the colour of containers.
An old freighter with
a beard of rust
lay anchored
in midstream.
Gulls flew between
the masts of moored ships.
Huge wharf cranes
walked the water's edge.
Into my hand they lowered an island.

From *Breeze*.

At Foodtown with the dog

CHARLOTTE GRIMSHAW

The dog and I roar towards Foodtown. We pull into the carpark as two Samoans are levering themselves out of their rusting two-tone Chrysler Valiant. They watch, munching drumsticks from a family bucket of Kentucky Fried Chicken as I drag the dog out of the passenger seat. The dog is four years old, an aggressive beast of an Alsatian with short bristly hair. Howard likes to rape, pillage, maim and generally screw up any other dog which strays into his path. With humans he likes to lick, purr, slobber, ingratiate and beg for food. I have become adept at breaking up the most spectacular dogfights. No canine brawl is too bloody for me. When Howard has eluded me on a peaceful beach, or snapped his lead in a cosy shopping mall, and immediately instigated an appalling argument with two Rottweilers, a Dobermann and three bull terriers, while the scene erupts in screams, roars, baying and moaning from dogs and owners alike, I don't hang back. I jump in. The trick is to take off all one's jewellery to avoid catching it on a collar or tooth, then get behind Howard's back as he's fastened to the other dog's throat, and yank him out by the collar and tail in one short, sharp heave from behind. It's the yank on the tail that releases his jaws. It's not bravery that makes me jump into the snarling teeth and flying fur, it's not lack of fear. It's just that I like the maul of it. I like the action. I long for a bit of heat.

Leaving the dog to rage and piss his way around the carpark, I head for the aisles. The supermarket is packed with the usual crowd, mostly Pacific Islanders, their trolleys groaning with tins of corned beef, coconut milk and packages of white bread. Irritated that the place is so crowded I force my way through the sweaty hordes. As I queue, wincing, at the fruit and vegetable stands, I reflect that only Pacific Islanders are huge enough and united enough in their perpetual merriment to be able to inflict ear pain with their laughter. Why are they so big? Why are they so amused? Deafened by the blasts of twenty-eight-stone hilarity at the paw-paw stand I head distractedly towards the delicatessen. Abandoning cultural sensitivity altogether I wonder how an entire section of the community can have let itself get so extraordinarily overweight. I know it's a sign of status in the Islands to be really enormous – at school Pacific Island girls snacked on whole loaves of bread split down the middle and filled with ice-cream, while we looked on faint with dieting – but what about things like fitness, nutritional awareness, full-fibre food?

But then again, those big Island girls found us risible too, with our miserable little bodies, our weird inhibitions. And look at them now, wheeling round the shelves, even fatter and laughing even harder. I had one sad friend in particular who would have caused them great mirth, a recovering anorexic; she was hospitalised once, so the story went, after inhaling the crouton she was having for dinner.

A traffic accident occurs, a huge, aggressive old guy ramming his creaking trolley into my leg. He frowns after me with heavy, ponderous authority as I make my way evilly round the store, small, pallid, my mind full of complaint and abuse, full of all those thoughts you can't articulate if you want to be right on, culturally sensitive, sane. When I emerge with my trolley the dog is crouched by the Porsche mumbling secretively into an ancient and soggy Kentucky Fried Chicken packet, which he tries to smuggle into the car for the journey home.

Disgusting hound, vile dog, I mutter as I dispose of his prize.

From *Provocation*.

A Grey Lynn story

JOHN PULE

Potau now spent most of his days at the TAB in Grey Lynn. From Monday to Friday I caught a bus out to Otahuhu. I started work at a new job at 8 am working in a factory packing light bulbs and got home at 6.30 pm.

A family down the road bought a snooker table and soon Niueans and Samoans were playing every night. On Thursday, payday, we played until the sun emptied the dew. I didn't go to work on Fridays for three months. Only then did the boss notice. I was fired and glad to leave all that shit behind. Soon I found a job working in Kingsland at the Kiwi bacon factory. That was my life. Nothing much in it, work and walk. Pay for rent, power, contribute to food. My mum had moved into my sister and her husband Dan's new home in Wiri. That area was known by everybody as Otara, but so many people were embarrassed that the name Otara signified booze, fights, unemployed, it came to be known as Wiri.

Mata had met a Samoan at a dance. His family had lived in a small house in East Tamaki since 1953. His father could not believe that his eldest son would go outside the fa'a Samoa and marry a Niuean. He pulled his hair out when he heard Mata was pregnant. That did not stop them. Dan believed in the philosophy of American movies like *Gunfight at the OK Corral*, or the John Wayne movies where the hero, with very few words, makes his point and stands up to the enemy. Well, Dad was like that, standing up to his father, his hands shivering where, if he were in a movie, his holster would be.

Hey man, some would say, wats ta matta, you liva ina Otara? Need da passport to enta da place. It's a strange country on its own – square boxes. Keith Hay homes springing out of the earth like unheard-of plants. My mum went to bless the house with her motherly air. I helped move their furniture to the new house. They could not wait until the soil settled down to a flat surface. Car tracks the size of one-year-olds obscured the base of the house. Like thousands of others, they sprayed grass seed. We struggled to lift the fridge over the mud. The glass front door opened into the lounge, into a little L-shape as the dining room turned into a small kitchen. The back door went down some concrete steps. Next to the kitchen a small washbasin. A small hallway and the three bedrooms went off this; at the end of the hallway was the bathroom and toilet. The wallpaper was dull white, but soon portraits of Potau and Lamahina went up; grandparents, children. Lamahina stayed out there for nearly six months, helping look after the kids, washing and hanging the clothes out, cooking and changing nappies of the youngest one.

Potau collected the benefit and walked back and forth to the TAB. He was settling down to a quiet life. When the grandchildren appeared on the horizon he came alive and bought litres of ice cream, soft drinks, bags of sweets for every child. Lamahina settled down to crocheting pillowcases with red and yellow hibiscus flowers, sometimes getting me to write words like Niue on the pillow or Love is at Home. She stitched each one with cotton.

One summer our house was painted green by our landlord. I never knew we had a landlord, a palagi. He turned up with men in dirty overalls and put up scaffolds around the house so it looked as though we were caged in. Lamahina was upset, as was Potau. It was not our house and we felt small, sitting in the house knowing that we had no say in what was happening around us. It hit home that the house belonged to someone else, as we sat silently for brief periods listening to the sound of paint-brushes sweeping the outside walls. Staring at each other, not knowing what it felt like to own something as big as a house.

Potau enlarged a photo of Thomas wearing his championship belt and hung it next to a photograph of me. It was around this time that he began reading the Bible and attending church every Sunday. Lamahina went along, not having any idea what all the commotion was about, only that going to these functions implemented changes. Everyone went along, lost, uncertain.

Every Thursday, Friday and Saturday nights I went out with the boys, coming back to a house that smelled of paint – living in a green house amused my cousins, who called us the Kermit family. Potau pulling weeds up and Lamahina washing tea-towels was a common sight. She never let the clothes pile up, hand-washed everything. Potau complained about the amount of water she used for one item of cloth. The fragrance of Sunlight soap drifted in and out of the house.

From *Burn My Head in Heaven.*

Coffee and cheese with Gudrun and Ursula

ANNA JACKSON

An afternoon moon sat in the sky the day
I wore my turquoise Mary Jane sandals away

from Minnie Cooper on Ponsonby Road. I
threw my scuffed sneakers into a bin and went to buy

a lattè from Byzantium. I sat outside where everyone
would see my sandals. I recognised Ursula and Gudrun

at once from D H Lawrence's *Women in Love* but didn't expect
them to acknowledge me till I noticed they too had picked

turquoise Mary Jane sandals to wear. Gudrun of course wore
them with rose red tights, Ursula with yellow ones, or

saffron to be precise, a green velvet skirt, and blouse
I recognised from window shopping at Wallace Rose.

We sat together drinking coffee and laughing at D
H Lawrence and I liked them more than ever free

of his prose. 'Oh look at the shoes!' cried a Japanese
tourist, and took a photo of us saying 'cheese'.

Way out west

MAURICE GEE

Westwards became our direction. I fight the urge to become adjectival. The coast out there crushes language flat. South of Muriwai is Anawhata. Then Bethells Beach, Piha, Karekare, Whatipu. That says enough for me and it's enough for Rex, although if you look at his poems you'll find words that mean the same. We came at a walking pace down the twisting roads, with the Beezer ticking and creaking, and an expectation in our minds of sea and cliff and sand – movement overturning on itself, height leaning in and leaning out, the body overturning, the mind starting to fall – desire, revelation, perhaps death. This becomes far too explicit. Rex can do this sort of thing without coming out. (See 'Bethells Beach', see 'Comber'.) We lay on the hot black sand and body surfed in the waves, and went out several times in winter and stood as close to the surf as we dared and climbed on the rocks and asked the seventh wave to take us. Once we swam, midwinter, all alone at Bethells, naked in the waves that overtopped us like walls and we came out like old bait, with the blood washed out of us, and trembled and stood bent long after we had pulled our clothes on. Our wrinkled hands could not tie our bootlaces up.

He took his sisters there, one by one, and would have taken Lila but she refused to ride on the bike. A kind of fatalism came on her when he was driven home one night skinned from his wrists to his elbows after a fall. Lumps of skin were nipped from his kneecaps and his ribs. I talked with Lila at the gate. 'I can't do any more, Jack. I can't care any more or I'll go mad.' She kept on caring, of course, but damped down her ways of expressing it, and went a little mad in a self-denying way.

Rex took me riding on the Scenic Drive, Swanson to Titirangi and halfway back, the night before I caught the Limited to Wellington. We stopped at the lookout and Auckland lay spread flat, winking its lights. 'Jesus,' I said, 'Wellington' (which I had never seen), 'I must be mad.'

'What does your old lady say?'

'She wants me to be a lawyer. Even doctors aren't good enough.'

'It's only a year, eh. Then you can come back.'

'If I come back I've got to live with her.'

'Who says?'

'Wellington's the only way I'll ever get away.'

He lit a cigarette and flicked the match away – down to Loomis, under the hills. 'I'm leaving home too. I'm getting a room in town.'

'Why?'

'Time is.' He grinned. 'I'm not going to stay too long like you.'

'You've got more than I have,' I said bitterly.

'That's just the way it turned out.'

We plunged down Forest Hill Road into Loomis. I was drunk with leaning over when we reached my gate. Light-headedness, and falling locked together, enclosed in our hard cell of light, made me say, 'I know how you feel, Rex.'

'Yeah?'

'My father and your sister, eh? It happened to us both.'

'Shut up, Jack.' His words came easily. But I had seen a pulse, a contraction, in his eyes, more than the street lamp could have made. He was enraged at my claim for equality; and then he was calm and put me off, tapping with his gloved fist on my shoulder. 'Take it easy down there. Keep in touch.' He pulled his goggles on and rode away.

It was six months before I saw Rex Petley again.

From *Going West*.

Henderson

CK STEAD

Two days later she called for him and they drove to Henderson, taking the new (or new to him) north-western motorway that ran out from Point Chevalier to North Te Atatu across some of the inner harbour's shallow tidal bays. There were horizontal striations of colour – olive-green mangroves, white sand, yellow mud, blue water – and such skimming, water-level views, long and clear down the miles of the harbour, it was as if the eye was drawn over it, fast, with the graph of the city skyline showing up on one side, and on the other the summit of Rangitoto, an inquisitive neighbour, looking over the fence the low-lying land made between Mt Victoria and North Head.

Seen from sea level, or equally from above, Auckland had a way of simplifying itself into patterns of land and water; and Mike was reminded of those paintings in Marica's house that had surprised him with their fresh abstractions of form and colour. That it was a beautiful location seemed to him true beyond question, and it was only a pity it had been inhabited, not by a race of gods, but by fallible mortals, first the Maori, who had called it the Place of a Thousand Lovers but made of it an inter-tribal killing field, then the Pakeha, who seemed hell-bent on turning it into a thoroughfare.

Everywhere now they were invaded, Mike especially, because he'd been away so long, but Marica too, by the recollections that are hidden, like traps waiting to be sprung, in the places of childhood and youth. They turned off the motorway at Te Atatu Road and stopped at Bridge Avenue where he'd so often 'doubled' her on his bike for a swim. The water flowed there still, under the motorway – in with the tide, out with the flow of the Whau River – and there was a marina, and many yachts moored to poles.

They went on up Te Atatu Road, identifying old houses, trying to remember what had been there before the new ones had been built. Everywhere orchards, vineyards and farmland had been subdivided and sold, to be replaced by suburban houses and gardens. They parked where once there had been the gate with the sign LICENSED TO SELL TWO GALS, and walked down the hill to stand silent, side by side, looking into the grounds of the school he and Frano had gone to. The buildings Mike had known, one in concrete, the other in white weatherboard, both with high-pitched ceilings and sash windows, were gone, replaced by undistinguished prefabs. But the setting, blue hills in the background, stream running past the lower grounds and under the road, was unchanged, and he was overwhelmed by its familiarity, as if he had come around a corner and run headlong into his long-dead mother.

Back in the car they drove to Waikumete, through the main gates, Marica following the path she knew would take them to the place where her family had their graves. The cemetery stretched away over rolling land, a city of the dead whose urban sprawl, Mike reflected, should make its inhabitants feel at home. They passed the crematorium building where a caretaker, enacting a haiku, was sweeping up rose petals from the front courtyard with a brush and pan. Everywhere the graves were adorned with fresh flowers and coloured plastic windmills, making him think of *le jour des morts*, the day of the year in France when everyone remembers and visits the graves of their dead. But in fact, Marica explained, Waikumete was like this every day, since the flowers left at the crematorium after each service were gathered up before the next and distributed around the graves.

They went over a hill, down into a hollow, and then

climbed the other side where tombs, strange to Mike, were built on either side of the narrow roadway – square or oblong box structures in marble or stone or plastered concrete, each like an infant-school drawing of a house, with a heavy iron door right in the middle, and two 'windows' of black marble, one on either side of the door. In large letters over the door was the name of the family to whom the tomb belonged – Marsich, Boracich, Frankovic, Dragicovic, Nobilo, Radich, Stipe, Marinkovic – some of them decorated with patterns of vines or of interlocking oak leaves. The names of the internees were inscribed on the black windows over the words '*Pocivali* (or *Pocivala*, or *Pocivao*) *u miru*' – the Croatian form, Marica explained, of Rest in Peace. Among them was a tomb with the name Selenich over its door.

'I don't remember these,' Mike said as he got out of the car and walked along what seemed like a street of pretend houses, reinforcing his earlier thought about a city of the dead.

'They weren't here then,' she said. 'That's prosperity for you, Mike. It brings on the pharaoh syndrome.'

'Will you be put in there?'

'Oh no. I'll be cremated. I don't think the dead should take up space. Of course if you could see through black marble, it's

92

what a real estate agent would call a prime position. We're like the Maori. We like a view of the sea for our dead.'

He turned and looked where she was looking, and there, sure enough, was a long view to the harbour and all the way down it to the city skyline ten kilometres away, the business towers and the hump of the harbour bridge standing out clear in morning light. And then, as his eye ranged about, near and far, he looked down the slope they were on, beyond the houselike tombs, over an area of lawn cemetery, all plaques inset flat into mown grass, to a neglected hollow where weeds and rank grass had grown up around older tombstones. He turned to her. 'Frano's down there.'

She smiled. 'So you remember.'

'And over there was where …' He didn't go on, but pointed away to the left. Most of the pines were gone, but there was a grove still standing.

She half nodded and turned away. It was just an acknowledgement, no more than that, but it was enough.

Back at the car she opened the boot and took out a trowel, a rake, a small shovel, a scrubbing brush, some plants in plastic pots. 'Help me, Mikie,' she said, and together they carried all this down into the shadowy hollow and walked about there, swishing

93

through weeds and grasses, scraping at headstones, calling out dates to one another, until they found a line of graves dated 1952, and among them, Frano's.

'Frano Heta Panapa,' Mike read. '1933–1952. Dearly Loved and Always Remembered Son of Ljuba Maria Panapa (née Selenich) and the late Joseph Parata Panapa. *Pocivao u miru.*' There was a photograph of Frano, faded now, water-stained, inset under perspex in the concrete headstone. A passage from the Psalms, 'O God, thou art my God, early will I seek thee', was repeated in Maori, 'E te Atua, noku koa Atua; ka moata taku rapu i a koe', and in Croatian, '*O Boze, ti si Bog moj; gorljivo tebe trazim.*'

To Marica, who was standing at his shoulder, Mike intoned, 'O Dog thou art my Dog, early will I seek thee.'

She smiled and put a hand on his arm. 'You two were such silly boys.'

The small plot in front of the headstone had been neglected, and for half an hour or more they worked on it, weeding, loosening the soil inside the concrete perimeter, putting in the shrubs and ferns and flowers Marica had brought, scrubbing dirt and moss from the stone, clearing the long grass from round about that might close in and engulf it

94

again. They were pleased with their work, it looked very good, and they took photographs, he of her, she of him, standing beside the grave.

'Ljuba will be pleased,' Mike said.

'Imagine if Frano could see us. What would he say?'

'He'd say fuck off, wouldn't he?'

'Yes, I suppose he would. But he wouldn't mean it. He'd be pleased.'

'You used to be scared of him.'

'Frano? No, never.'

'That's how it seemed.'

'I was scared of hurting him. Hurting his feelings. You didn't understand that, Mike, and I never felt as if I could explain it to you.'

As she said that she looked puzzled, and young. Her youthful face showed through for a moment, like a face at a window, and then the curtain of the present came down. Mike stared at her.

'What is it?' she asked.

'What's what?'

'You were looking at me as if …'

'I was remembering.'

'Oh.' She waved him away. 'Don't do that.'

'Knocked down by a speeding memory in the city of the dead.'

He turned and looked towards what remained of the pines. He would have liked to go there, hunting for the place where they'd first made love, but he didn't suggest it.

That evening they went together to a restaurant in Parnell and then drove along the waterfront to sit in the car looking out across the water where Rangitoto appeared and faded as the moon moved fast and purposeful as a sheep dog through flocks of cloud. They held hands.

'Life's a bitch,' he said, after a silence that had lasted so long he wasn't sure what he meant.

'Only if you think it is,' she said; and he silently rebuked himself for a lapse in his Zen discipline.

'Are you still a Catholic?' he asked.

'Are you still a New Zealander?'

'It's like that, is it?'

'It's not a question of believing.'

'Of loyalty?'

'Not even that.'

'Identity?'

She laughed at his persistence. 'I suppose ... Yes. Identity will do.'

From *Talking About O'Dwyer*.

Going west

Maurice Gee

Black lands. Navy-blue. Earth-brown. Clay-yellow. Ochrous. Brackenish. Brackish. Creek-green. These are words he chooses for his west. That west out there that makes him uneasy because it is where he grew up and where a part of him still belongs. He wants to leave no parts lying around.

Down again, along, through, into. Here is Loomis under the hills. A glass and tile front, traffic lights and carparks and people. He wants the town of empty dusty streets and broken hedges. It's in behind and a long way back. He drives down the shopping streets and turns left into industry and commerce – where once a little square-built jam factory had stood – and passes through a district of panel-beating shops and coal and firewood yards and boarded-up stores until, at a straggly line, Loomis is residential. It's Polynesian too, and he drives carefully. There was only one Maori at Loomis school when he was there. Now, he has read in the *Herald*, a third of the pupils are Maoris and Islanders.

Women in muu-muus talk on a lawn. Youths with dread-locked hair stand around a stripped-down motorbike. He's anxious that they shouldn't notice him. They are foreign, he is foreign – who owns the point of view? He sees how his presence in this street, his clothes, his car, his language, speech, habits of mind, can only provoke. Is there any part of Loomis he can claim as his own? And backwards-claiming – what can it signify in the Loomis-1990 world? He feels that he is doing something vaguely indecent.

He drives on all the same, and goes down a hill into a neighbourhood that seems pakeha. Across a concrete bridge where once a wooden… Along the road, beside the creek where once… Unseemly word; 'once' prevents, doesn't it, good mental health? Yet it creates a country, it's a territory in his brain. Jack declares his right to go there.

He parks, he locks his car, he tries to find his old swimming hole. The creek is opened up. It's as if someone has forced two hands into the gorge and pulled it wide. The creek lies in the sun. It never did that except at midday. But it's dirtier and meaner. That is natural. The water in the hole is yellow-green. It has a rotting vegetation smell in place of the eel smell he remembers. There's nothing for him here, no folding together of now with memory. Jack sneezes once and turns away. He climbs back to the roadside and finds two youths looking at his car. They must have come down from the houses over the street. One wears a league jersey and the other a cotton T-shirt with the arms torn off. League is threat. Torn off is threat. Jeans. Boots. Shaven heads. Beer cans that gurgle in unison.

'Lost something, mate?'

'No, no, I'm just looking around.'

'Good idea to lock your car round here.'

They have seen him do it. Jack blushes, half in fright. 'It's just a habit.'

'Good idea. Might get your stereo knocked off, eh?'

'Ha ha ha,' the other laughs.

'I was looking at the creek,' Jack says. 'I grew up in a house along the road. I used to swim in the pool down there.'

'Yeah?'

'Fifty years ago.'

They cannot comprehend fifty years. All the same they soften. They have drunk enough beer to make them sentimental. 'I had a raft there. When I was a kid.'

'Yes?'

'We piled the rocks up, eh? We made a real big pool.'

'It's a good creek,' the other says. 'I learned to swim down there.'

'So did I,' Jack says, although it's a lie. He learned to swim at Cascade Park. 'There were great big eels.'

Their eyes swing on to him. It's plain the eels have gone. He had better be careful not to make his creek better than theirs. But he's moved to find they have a creek at all. He is moved that it's still alive.

'It's deeper than I remember.' Another lie, but a gift to them.

'She's deep, all right. There's a pool up there you can't touch the bottom. I used to try.' The league jersey youth turns away. He's as moved as Jack.

'Have a beer, mate,' the other says.

'I'd better not. I'm driving.' He's envious of someone diving deep in his creek and wants to ask the young man what he found down there. He stamps his foot on the road. 'When I lived here this was all gravel and dust.'

'Musta been a long time ago.' They are not interested in the road. They walk to the creek edge and look at the water. 'Good creek.'

'Thanks for talking to me.'

'No sweat.'

'I'd better get along the road and see my old house.'

'Remember to keep your car locked.'

'Ha ha ha.'

Nice boys, he thinks as he drives away. He wants to keep them simple; doesn't want to look at their lives. That way they don't interfere but share the creek. He goes around two bends and finds a grassed area where there had been a field of gorse. He never penetrated it and never came to the creek that way. Now he can walk down and stand on the rocks by the water and make out a bike frame and bottles in the mud. He can turn and run his eye up the slope and over the road and get a partial view of the house he had lived in for the first twenty years of his life.

Partial because although the row of pine trees is cut down two new houses stand where the summer-house and the rose garden used to be. He sees the old front porch and door framed between decramastic roofs and hardiplank walls. The curving drive is gone – where is the curve, where is the contour, that stand for the times he got away? Running down the drive, leaning on the curve, bent him out of her world into his. Now there is a right-of-way between wire fences, running from the road to the door. There would have been no escape on that narrow way.

Jack sneezes four times. (It's nowhere near his record of

nineteen, brought on by the smell of animals in the Wellington zoo.) He blows his nose on tissues and wads them into a ball, which he fires at a cairn of stones on the far bank, and hits it square. That gives him the confidence to look at the house again. It was built in 1927 for the newlyweds and the mortgage was paid off in 1947, several weeks before Walter Skeat made his fatal dismount from the train. They had their twentieth wedding anniversary there, though no one celebrated or even mentioned it. Dorothy Skeat – had anyone ever called her Dot? – stayed on in the house until the mid sixties, when she sold it for a very nice price and bought a home unit in Epsom. Jack had last seen the house as she moved out: four-square and substantial at the end of its white-shell drive.

Now, the letterboxes say, it is divided into flats. 126A, B, C, D. How can four families, even four couples, fit in there? Another question – what made the Skeats think they needed so much space? Four bedrooms, two bathrooms, two living-rooms, a dining-room, a study, for three people? It only started to make sense when you understood that each of those three people lived alone.

From *Going West*.

Lone Kauri Road

ALLEN CURNOW

The first time I looked seaward, westward,
it was looking back yellowly,
a dulling incandescence of the eye of day.
It was looking back over its raised hand.
Everything was backing away.

Read for a bit. It squinted between the lines.
Pages were backing away.
Print was busy with what print does,
trees with what trees do that time of day,
sun with what sun does, the sea
with one voice only, its own,
spoke no other language than that one.

There wasn't any track from which to hang
the black transparency that was travelling

south-away to the cold pole. It was cloud
browed over the yellow cornea which I called
an eyeball for want of another notion,
cloud above an ocean. It leaked.

Baldachin, black umbrella, bucket with a hole,
drizzled horizon, sleazy drape,
it hardly mattered which, or as much
what cometing bitchcraft, rocketed shitbags,
charred cherubim pocked and pitted the iceface
of space in time, the black traveller.
Everything was backing away.

The next time I looked seaward,
it was looking sooted red, a bloodshot cornea
browed with a shade that could be simulated
if the paint were thick enough, and audible,
to blow the coned noses of the young kauri,
the kettle spout sweating,
the hound snoring at my feet,
the taste of tobacco, the tacky fingers
on the pen, the paper from whose plane

the last time I looked seaward
would it be a mile, as the dust flies,
down the dulling valley, westward?
everything was backing away.

From *Trees, Effigies, Moving Objects.*

Bred in South Auckland

GLENN COLQUHOUN

I drive a car that is falling apart.
There is bog in the body.
There is rust in the doors.
Occasionally it does not have a warrant.
Sometimes I sleep in large rooms full of people.
I eat too much fried bread.
I am late to meetings.
I go to housie.
My nose is flat.
I say Raw – tore – loo – uh.

Some people think I am a bloody maori.

I have been to university.
I have a student loan.
I photocopy my tax returns.

Most mornings I read the newspaper.
I make lists of things I have to do and like to cross them off.
I cut apples into quarters before I eat them,
Then I cut the pips out.
I put my name on things.
I listen to talkback radio.
I use EFTPOS.

Some people think I am a typical pakeha.

Last week I drove through a red light,
I did not slow down at a compulsory stop,
I changed lanes on the motorway and did not use my indicator.
When I was a boy I went to see *Enter the Dragon*,
I took one lesson in kung fu.
My parents made me do my homework.
My brother gave me chinese burns.
I like beef and pork flavoured two minute noodles.
I light incense when the house smells.
Once I dug a garden.

Some people think I am a blasted asian.

When I was a boy I learnt to swear in Samoan,
I went to school in Mangere.
I played rugby in bare feet,
Sometimes I shop at the Otara markets.
My family come from overseas.
I used to work in a factory.
Once I helped to cook an umu.
When it is summer I wear a lavalava.
I drink pineapple juice.
I like to eat corned beef.

Some people think I must be a flaming coconut.

I think I am the luckiest mongrel I know.

From *The Art of Walking Upright.*

The biggest Polynesian city in the world

JOHN PULE

We moved from house to house. Sackville Street. Rose Road. Richmond Road. Potau was drinking Thursday payday, Friday, Saturday. The fights over nothing led us to flee many times during the night, walking miles in the misty nights to knock quietly on relatives' doors.

Lamahina's brother Aki lived in Newmarket. The house shook when the trains went past. I learned that a certain sound opened the horizon and I ran out down to the railway tracks. An old palagi was concerned and stood by my side. Lamahina screamed and was at my other side, thanking the man in broken English while dragging me back inside. —Don't play here or Potau will see you. The house we were hiding in was just across the road from the Hollywood, one of many pubs the Niuean men frequented. We stayed there for months, Potau not knowing where we lived.

Nogi asked Lamahina to go back to her brother who was wasting away with momoko and sadness that his children were not by his side. Aki wanted to go and beat Potau to a pulp. One time Fetu and cousins beat him up right there in front of his wife. After six months we went back to Potau. For one month the Richmond Road house knew peace and harmony. Then Potau came home by taxi, stood outside, drunk, rolling in the air, cursing us. He beat Lamahina in the bedroom. Us kids ran up and down the hallway until Mata ran outside. Later the police took Potau away.

Aifai took to drinking too. The poet. Church was all white. Repent before a certain time. Pray. Nogi kept coming around to talk to Potau who nodded in agreement. I looked at Lamahina, sitting there, studying the carpet ripped to shreds by the constant moving of chairs, exposing squashed cockroaches, dust, beer bottle-tops and a dirty wooden floor. The sun never reached the lounge. The natural light, at its strongest at the window, faded quickly to pitch black. The leis lost their colours and a coat of grease layered them. A photo of Liku church in one corner. A couch. Two big purple chairs. The wallpaper an earth brown. The hearth was never used, but the floor was burned in several areas resembling black eyes. Leading into the kitchen, wallpaper peeled away and hung listlessly. A stove covered in black grease was close, too close to the sink.

One night Aifai came home with Potau. I was asleep in one

of the two rooms. My room when the curtains were drawn was dark, curly like doll's hair.

I heard them outside the door. A pause to step in, then their voices loud and louder still. I recognised Lamahina's walk as she came out of her room. Her footsteps were subdued, frightened, lost, wandering in her own house. I heard Aifai yelling. Two uncles walked in. I recognised their voices as Tamauka and Hiva. Quiet. Aifai was telling a story. Lamahina shouted, —Siake la e tau mena ea, kua mole tei.

My family has something about the past. It is a place where they stage their battles and skirmishes. The house shakes. Heavy movements, shifting shoes, a crash, yelling, silence.

I sit up in bed. I don't like the sudden sound. Words. Niue. Aifai is talking again, his voice sliding down a mountain ripped apart by bulldozers. Whatever happened after that was what shook the hallway. Photos fell to the floor. I rushed out to see Potau on the ground, blood pouring out of his mouth and eye. I arrived in time to see Aifai hit the old man over the head with a chair. Lamahina covered Potau with her arms while Hiva pushed Aifai outside. I watched them tumble out the front door, the red stained glass reflecting distorted figures. The door was sick. Must be. People in and out, in and out.

I glimpse a bit of the road, where a lady is watching. Lamahina is crying. Potau gets up. Tamauka walks in. I approach the three and am told to go back to my bedroom.

Instead I walk out on to the street, and look back with a group of palagi. What is all this? I notice the house is different. Paint has long ago wasted away, and the walls are almost black, stained by rain and sun. The police turn up. I follow. Questions. Broken words. The cops leave. Nogi visits that evening, loudly saying that this is New Zealand and this sort of behaviour is not wanted. She scolds Potau about his attitude in front of the children, his wife.

We did not see Aifai again until a wedding reception at the Manhattan in Mount Roskill. A Niuean band played rock and roll songs, a few Elvis numbers which brought the young people up to a slow rhythm. The bride was floating around the guests, figita, hongi. As usual the men got together and it was not long before the fire was fed with more wood. Aifai sat solemnly. Potau carried on content that the man who bashed him over the head had a problem. Potau told him to shut up and listen. Hiva urged Potau to tell a story, a legend. Fetu showed off and sank a glass of whisky down; Mila and Jack were already pissed.

Potau stood up and said, —I'd like to dedicate this story to the tama vale. Everyone stared at Aifai, who stood up and walked out of the function.

This is the story rarely heard these days. It begins in a village on the Motu side. A sister gave birth to a baby and her brother hearing the good news visited with food and water. For some reason the sister would not show the brother the baby's face. Stranger still, the baby was encouraged from an early age to live alone in a house some distance away. It was a well-kept secret as the baby was never human. She had given birth to an eel. When the brother visited his sister with food, the eel confronted him at the door. The brother turned to run and the eel called out, –You can't leave in a hurry, I want to eat you.

Like a brave Niuean the man ran for his life. The eel chased and caught up with the man who threw a comb at the creature. The eel stopped, combed its hair and continued the chase. When the eel caught up with the man he threw down some oil which spread neatly on the earth. The eel rested and gazed into the oil, admiring its hair and good looks. The eel once again chased the man who threw down a girdle. The eel was surprised to receive such an honour and tried on the girdle. The man was exhausted and had reached the ocean. When he thought the eel was satisfied, it appeared at his side with open jaws. The man jumped into the sea and turned into stone. Even today the stone image of the man is shown clinging to the reef.

Potau bowed. Mila came back with a bottle of whisky and filled all the glasses. Everybody cheered.

Fetu collapsed outside his house. He was carrying bags of fruit and pork bones. As he lifted his hand to open the door he saw a god hunting the fires he lit in the forest, spitting on them until smoke circled his eyes. Fetu was cremated so the spirits that lived in his mouth would burn with him. Goodbye.

During those summer days of beauty and singular sensations Aifai committed suicide by hanging himself. I forget the month. Before I knew what was happening we were at Aifai's funeral. The street was black. Latona was in black. A soft material covered her face although tears glittered on contact. He had hanged himself in the bathroom of their tiny Mount Eden flat. He managed to secure two belts to a ceiling pipe, balanced himself on the bath and jumped. The three-day wake was a nightmare. The bathroom was out of bounds. I poked my head in to see the bath, the greasy ceiling and the wet floor. It produced a feeling like a closet. Silent. Dark. Almost hypnotic. Potau whacked me.

Aifai had run from the Manhattan, then slowed down as his heart had demanded a body capable of swimming. To run down to the coast. Never mind the lights and pulsating houses listening to the wind presenting itself as a promise to your throat. Just run, somewhere, anywhere. People cannot hear what is rushing through his head. Only it is dangerous, maybe maybe not. It has a way of recognising hope. He walked all the way home. By then nothing in the world could make him change his mind. —I want to die, he kept saying. Over and over. —Potau, I hope you live to regret this night, this day, that you ever knew me as your son. I have had enough. I am going to die, now, tonight.

Every room in the tiny flat contained a dome of spotless windows. Even the hallway, a dumb space that petrified Thomas, secreted from its walls a sickly pus, that shook as if a great breath of air blew from the limbs of Aifai. So far away he thought, life is so far away. Thomas' face briefly appears as a tree, then Latona appears weeping in disbelief at what the windows were offering to Aifai as a farewell gift. Dogs that charged and barked at his loneliness. His eyes widened. He couldn't recognise the people moving furniture out of his way, yelling at crowds to disperse and let him walk unhindered. His pupils dilated some more. Nothing stood in his way. A voice obscured his thoughts as he reached for the belts. He must hurry.

Walking towards the bathroom. The pathway is clear. The room white. Lovely and white as the house. He throws the belt over the bar, loops a circle, balances on the bath and places it over his head until it rests on his neck. He tightens the belt. Tears burst from his eyes. He sees in the mirror his hands as he jumps and his head tilts sideways and looks to heaven.

I was attending Kowhai Intermediate School and missed the burial. Thomas was in college. We met mostly on weekends at Nogi's house. The atmosphere was strikingly strengthened by Aifai's death. Not strengthened as holding us together but the strength to force us to fall apart. It takes a lot of power to come together and not much to fall apart. Maybe in the years ahead the family would learn how to cope with conflicts or words that travel through the corpuscle new air.

From *Burn My Head in Heaven.*

Growing up at Point Chevalier

PETER WELLS

I grew up in a place that has a quite distinct geographical identity. This is because it is a small peninsula, with everything that is implied in that: the calm of insularity, the penile shape, I guess, of something pushing out into a harbour, or water. Historically the place was known as Rangi-mata-rau. Six years before Captain Cook first sighted New Zealand, the beach was the site of a fierce battle between Ngati Whatua and Ngati Paoa. My two friends (my brother Russell and Frankie, a tomboy who might as well have been our sister) and I played in a pit that was, quite possibly, a lookout from this early period. When I went back there forty years later I saw how it looked right up the harbour. We had chosen it, or found it, on our forays in the park. In our minds it was 'our bunker'.

We'd watched enough World War II movies for this to be the imprinting image on our brains. I'm not talking nostalgia here. I'm talking about something more primary, more necessary –

something cauterising and branding too, with the pain of something embedded in flesh. A tattoo perhaps, invisible to the eye, but still marking me out, confirming in me ways of doing, of seeing. Even ways of wincing at times. It's fascinating the way childhood feelings have a way of returning, on the long loop home.

If I grew up in the calmness of insularity, this for a long time appeared pleasing: self-contained, entire and, up to a point, complete. I accepted the terms of the world I grew up in, for a long while not really doubting things. Or perhaps the doubt came in the form of dreams. If I accepted what I saw in the daylight world, I was plunged at night into a chaotic, mysterious reality so powerful that it left me exhausted, seeming to have travelled great – emotional – distances. I never really saw the outside world in the same way again. I kept some private doubt.

My parents were like any young parents, hoping that the new generation could avoid the mistakes and messes of the old. That's impossible, of course – or at the very least, a big ask. Do I blame my poor old parents for what was so inexpertly hidden, yet placed so far at the back of the psychic drawer it has taken almost my entire lifetime for the truth to bleed out? Were they not doing what they thought was best? It was the way people behaved then. It was a different world.

It's impossible not to talk of politics. I grew up in the baby boom, which meant that in the same breath as supposedly being born into one of the luckiest generations of the twentieth century, we were also born on the cusp of a vanished war. The sounds of this trauma off-stage, tidily put to rest, seemed symptomatic of my childhood. Just as I had dreams of gargantuan yet very precise horror, so there had been horror on a global scale just five years before I was born. The Cold War was slicing everything into a schizoid division, neat as it was paranoid. I grew up unthinkingly conservative, racist, snobbish to an almost hallucinatory degree, rabid just as I was uncertain.

When it became apparent I was homosexual, I have to be honest and say I would never have known I was anything unusual at all, until it was pointed out with such assiduity, such disbelief, such ribaldry, such sharp and vindictive humour. With this new self-consciousness awarded to me, I became increasingly aware of a conflict between myself and the world I lived in. Perhaps it was symptomatic of the narrowness of my horizons, my constriction, that the world I lived in translated almost purely to Point Chevalier. By the time I was a teenager, the world that surrounded me was the rugby-league club, the tap-dancing class, Sunday school, the athletics club, scouts; yet none of these could answer my needs; indeed, each one of them served to exaggerate the one fact: I didn't seem to fit anywhere. Or I could only fit by trying to 'pass'. And I did try to pass. Desperately, for a long time. Of course if I had known how impossible this was – such a waste of time, such a terrible misuse of my youth – I would probably have given up on the spot. Many young people do. They kill themselves. I did think of this, broodily, in a typically teenage way – but I chose not to kill myself. I chose to go on living.

Many years later my mother could still be heard to say, blithely, 'Of course it was a wonderful place to grow up. There was everything there you could want.' And she would tick them all off on her fingers: the scouts, athletics, the church and swimming. It was perhaps only when my books began to appear, and she covertly read them, that a certain, embarrassed, even mystified silence would fall. I felt in her a kind of consternation. She was finding it difficult to match up her own view, or take on my childhood, with my view. Perhaps the sense of pain in my childhood shocked her.

One of the features my mother had ticked off, perhaps most resoundingly of all, was the beach. But in fact I stopped swimming, quite dramatically, at the age of twelve. This needs to be explained a little. To grow up at Point Chevalier, 'down the very bottom' as we would unself-consciously describe it, is to grow up with the sea. The peninsularity of the place is nowhere better expressed than in the feeling of a ship's prow riding out into the harbour. We who lived 'down the bottom of the Point', knew all sorts of secrets.

This had to do with the tides, the weather. Because if the area, on one level, was a banal collection of streets, set like a grid over hillocks, dips and what had once been paddocks, the most important element was that the sea existed on both sides of the peninsula, and at times the atmosphere of the sea, its pervasive moods, its storms or days of being becalmed, overtook the minutiae of bungalow and power pole, the cliché of tarseal and tin roof: we were plunged into another world.

Among the people who chose to live there – those who did choose – there was always an almost silent awareness that they lived somewhere special: a place on perennial holiday. It wasn't of course. It was a poorer suburb, full of people who worked hard to make a living. But if it was that, it had this other little rill, which was that everyone there dreamt, at least partially, or paid homage to the idea, of pleasure, of a life centred on what you wanted to do. The Point, down where we lived anyway, had a feeling of being a holiday place, improbably planted over the very ordinary domestic architecture of a poorer 1940s suburb. You saw this in the coloured rocks one of our neighbours placed around her garden, or the way she made her front lawn into a 'showplace' of annuals she obtained a little dubiously. The houses right down the bottom had a semi-defensive aspect to them because, in the early days – before affluence came in and people got their own cars – trolley buses would bring hundreds of people, even thousands on a hot weekend, to 'our end of the Point'.

This gave us both a proprietorial pride and a sense of superiority, even sovereignty. These people, we knew, would flood down onto the beach, or have their picnics; the shop 'down the bottom' had queues running out of it onto the footpath; the two separate lots of changing sheds would be full all day long; there might even be a distinct smell in the air, of melting tarseal and ice-cream: but we also knew these visitors – these tourists –

would depart. There would be the long, long months of autumn, and winter; during this time the Point became like a resort town abandoned. We spread ourselves out. The old maypole down on the beach and the swings in the municipal park would creak back and forth, no one much using them except ourselves, and we would only alight on them momentarily, like gulls, as Russell and Frankie and I considered what we would do next.

The very end of the Point, the bottom of the bottom (or the tip of the top, if you prefer, and this is probably how we saw it), was where my little band of friends grew up. The banks, the little riddling paths around the cliffs, the lookouts over the harbour, the beach itself, laced around with the slight melancholy of pohutukawa out of season: this was my playground – the anarchic, pleasurable, imaginary world of childhood.

The far stricter, more real one was the lines of lime burnt into grass that made the hundred-yard dash, or the insignia of knots I had to learn for scouts. I was slipping out of childhood into that harder knowledge, of being an adolescent. Adding to the difficulty was an inseparable truth: as I was placed in groups, so it became very clear that I was unusual, that I didn't have the right responses.

In time, as the teenagers around me all entered adolescence

at exactly the same time – and this was one of the un-thought-of effects of the baby boom – a kind of hormonal frenzy started to shake the suburb. A darker complexion entered. It was at this time I made a somewhat fatal decision: I decided I would not enter this unruly world in which there didn't seem a part for me. I turned my back, and went inwards. I stayed at home. I stayed inside the family. I can see now how fatal this was for me: I missed out on learning a lot of things that I could perhaps have blundered my way through. But I guess all I can say is this was how I survived.

My older brother, faced with exactly the same predicament, had taken a different route. He was homosexual also (and perhaps this is what made the outside world so difficult for me to contemplate, or make sense of – in our own reality, we were what was true). My brother chose, or couldn't stop himself from choosing, to voyage out into the real world. I grew up in a suburb where my brother's homosexuality, his availability, was notorious. This certainly did not help the snob in me. We had grown up thinking we were in some way superior to a lot of the working people in the suburb. We stood up when our elders entered a room, sat down at a table each night, we had a tablecloth, our parents never, for one moment, bashed each other up. In time these frugal arts of gentrification grew increasingly desperate. And it was perhaps at this time, when my family life became almost unendurably complex – yet when I seemed more than ever stuck within it, incapable of finding any way out – that the Point came to seem a nightmare, a spiritual graveyard.

I gave up swimming. Almost symbolically I turned my back on what I had loved as a child: the thing that made the Point unique. (Just as the bleeding away of the tide made the Point unique in another way – the vistas of mud, fringed with mangrove, guilty as pubic hair – this was one of our secret pleasures also.) At this time of extreme self-consciousness, I decided I could no longer allow myself the vulnerability of unwrapping my body in public. The eroticising of everything threatened me, just as it seduced me. The boys I desired were larrikins who I knew were only too willing to have some sort of rough, abrasive sex; I could survive the sex – but could I survive the name-calling? The semi-humorous but deeply humiliating yelling out of a name?

Perhaps my decision, at this stage, not to take on this burden led me later in life almost self-consciously (yet subconsciously) to brave another form of name-calling: to come out in public life earlier than many of my gay peers. (And I mean here coming out in the town you grew up in. The great cities of the world are full of brave men and women who are not out in their home towns. One of the tropes of Aids was the sophisticated man of the world, now ill, now dying, coming home from a great city to somewhere small and parochial, into a world that had no idea he was gay.)

Later, almost as a tic douloureux, a phobic way of allaying the ghosts of my childhood, I would be an out gay man. This was my irrevocable line of defence. So much pain, so much humiliation, so long a period sequestered, so lengthy a confinement in the prison of the closet – this meant as an adult I could never go back. The saying, then, that you can never go home again has a special meaning for me.

But aren't ambiguous feelings the reality of maturity? I hope this chapter has explained the complexity of feelings I hold for a place I simultaneously hate and love. The curve of the pohutukawa as they defy gravity and lean down the cliff, the marvellously ornate veins clinging to the clay banks, the faint track through the fallen pohutukawa leaves of the old paths around the cliff edges, the somnolence of a drip falling inside the changing rooms, the raw squeak of the swings as the wind moves them about in autumn or winter, the prairie plain of Point Chevalier Road by night, when everyone is asleep and I'm still driving around the suburb looking for something lost or mislaid – all of these are veins of my personality that still pump, resoundingly, blood.

But of course there are problems trying to speak out in your own home town. My mother still lives in Auckland, though she resolutely changed her suburb when she was at long last able. (But even for her the Point remains a central reference: where we lived our family life perhaps. Our history lies there: the body of it, the pulverised bones.)

Trying to talk about your own family and personal history in this narrow context is difficult, even at times impossible. What can I say? The murmuring voices of the past say: *be silent*, let the pain be absolved in the great balm that is time. But time is also pressing. Although we lived 'down the road' from the biggest mental asylum in the country, we never for one moment considered that we had anything to do with insanity. We were sane: anyone who crossed that boundary and went in through the gates was insane. It was that stark and simple.

At times I feel like the Ancient Mariner who 'yet must tell his tale'. Increasingly, I guess, gay men and women wish to distance themselves from the past and project an adamantine surface of sexiness and success. In this world, to look back is to risk turning, not to stone, but to the uncertain being we all once were – the unformed being, the person without the smart comeback, the one without an answer. But this is where we all started from. Most people do.

In the end, though, I think that while my story is individual, as anyone's is, each moment of decision is a juncture in a route to an adult identity. My story is also part of a time, a place, a period. It is, in some senses, personal history, but the emphasis has to be on the second part of the equation: *history*.

As I said at the beginning, you tend to have two different viewpoints of where you grow up. My childhood view was so adhesively close to the Point and its many moods that I unthinkingly loved it. Maybe I had no choice – certainly I didn't have much of a sense of comparison. Perhaps it's a symptom of my advancing age that I more and more lull and return to that first view I had of the place: the Point. Is it an irony that the place I came from, the place I started out from, the place that defined me and formed me perhaps more than any other, was actually called the Point? This is what we true locals all called it anyway.

Maybe in the end then this is what I learnt, what I got: I came to understand the Point.

Even as recently as a year ago, I gave a talk in Wellington and described some black-and-white photos of my Point Chevalier childhood, saying, 'One is overwhelmed by a sense of space, emptiness, silence. In our suburban world of white weatherboards and blank sky, my brother and I stared into the camera and waited for life to start happening – to become real – so we could awaken. We seemed to have no gay images at all – none that we could apply to ourselves. In fact when I think of my childhood – and knowledge of gayness – I think of silence, absence, unknowingness, and the lack of connection between an inner voice and … the real world where homosexual men and women did exist and lived ordinary lives – loved, fell out of love, got bored, did the shopping, wrote letters, slept, dreamt, made love and went to work. This world was carefully screened from us – by our parents, and by the wider society. Yet the fact is, this other life was happening all the time …'

The extraordinary thing is I myself had managed to render into that white chalk dust of oblivion the fact that Laurie featured all through my childhood. True, I was no longer a child when she was killed. I was a teenager. But, retrospectively, this showed that all along there had been homosexual people in my childhood – people who did shopping, visited, cracked jokes and gave presents – I just hadn't recognised them.

Is this another way of saying I was 'forgetting'? Or just that, as a child, I saw with different eyes?

From *Long Loop Home: A Memoir*.

Going home

STEPHANIE JOHNSON

In Mechanics Bay the scow waited to unload her logs into the booms. After the Brynderwyn mountains the land surrounding the harbour seemed low, lumpy and dull. Wet to the skin, William leaned his aching arms in the stern and took in the city of his birth, grey under the slow spitting sky. Tin-roofed wooden houses clung to the ridges that led away from the shambles on the shore. Further around from Mechanics Bay, out of sight now, was the solid respectable vein of Queen Street, which fed the rest of the city's ragged body. On previous returns, William had longed for Queen Street, the upper half of it, its bars and bawdy-houses, but now the odour of the marsh filled his nostrils. The place was just a swamp, with a series of volcanic mounds rising on the horizon. There was never a more ridiculous place to build a city. It invited failure, a drowning in mud or death from a cataclysm of boiling rock. No wonder he had never thrived here, he thought. Even without catastrophe, swamp-gas mixes with the salt air and depresses the inhabitants' spirits.

Late in the afternoon, a dinghy came alongside the scow, carrying a company clerk to consign the cargo. William seized his opportunity, making his escape before the work was finished: he jumped aboard the small boat as the clerk, a weasly youth, took his leave. The skipper yelled abuse after him, his words lost on the gritty wind sloughing across the jumble of timber yards. In the dinghy's bow, William turned his back on him and wished he had a hat to ward off the chill. Winter was coming to Auckland too, the third deadening season he would have spent on the farm. He felt something like relief, mixed through with trepidation: he had no money and his father's wrath would be incalculable. At the slip he helped the clerk pull the dinghy up before taking off across the yard, along Customs Street and up Jacob's Ladder towards the Supreme Court.

At the bottom of Symonds Street he almost collided with an errand boy running down the steep hill, propelled forward by his burden of a crate of apples. The child's eyes widened in alarm the moment they rested on William's face. William brought a hand to his hair, felt how it had frizzled and crisped in the fire. There was a burn on his forehead that hurt under the weight of his

133

palm. He drew his shirt together and tried to close it over his vest. There were only two remaining buttons. The boy's gaping mouth annoyed him. He grabbed him by the arm.

'What are you gawping at?'

'You, Mister. You been in a war?'

William pulled the cap from the boy's head with his free hand, jammed it on his own head. Too small, but at least it went some way to hiding the burnt stubble.

'What day is it?' he asked suddenly. A smirk twisted the boy's lips.

'Friday.'

'Have you come from the court? Is Justice McQuiggan sitting?'

'No. Don't know. Give me back my cap, Mister.' The boy's skinny arms shifted under the crate: he wasn't strong enough to pull one out and make a lunge. William grabbed an apple in his wounded hand, bit into it and swallowed. The boy snivelled.

'I'll get in trouble.'

'Here.' William dug in his pocket, pulled out a coin. He dropped it down the boy's back and gave him a shove, sending him on his top-heavy way.

He wouldn't go to the court, then, but to the house. He

retraced his steps and made his way along Beach Road, under the railway bridge and up the hill. On Parnell Road women stood gossiping in shop fronts and the Windsor Castle was full. Outside St John's a knot of snot-nosed kids gazed at William, who slowed his pace when he drew level with the churchyard. The McQuiggans' house was clearly visible from here, cream-coloured and grand on the ridge parallel to Parnell Road, above a narrow bushy gully. High on its western wall a dormer window, set beneath the green raked-iron gable, caught the sun uncovered by a shifting cloud. It was early evening, not dark enough yet for the lamps to be lit. One of his sisters, or Henry, might be standing behind one of the second-storey panes, hidden by the glare, watching his slow progress up the hill.

He eschewed the front door, went around to the lane and looked over the gate. The door to the scullery stood open and Henry sat on the back step holding one of the cats, stroking it gently and whispering. It flicked its ears, its eyes half wild. William watched, waited for it to scratch and leap as they always did eventually, as they had all through Henry's childhood. His brother's head was bowed and William saw that he was beginning to go bald. Two years ago, when William had last seen him, he had seemed ageless, his unlined face a repository for his calm, happy disposition. He looked up suddenly, though William had made no movement. His face was unchanged. He stared at him for a moment, puzzled, his child-eyes wide, until William opened the gate. A roar of delight frightened the cat away and Henry was on his feet, wrapping his brother in his big arms.

'Will! Will!' he crowed, pulling the cap from William's head, kissing his cheek, his ear and his neck, his bristly face colliding with William's.

'Henry –' William made a grab for the cap.

Henry had taken his hands now and was skipping in a circle on the path, his big tummy bobbing above his belt until a movement on the step caught his eye. A brown skirt fell against its wearer's legs. Abruptly, he stood still.

'See, Ellen! See who has come!'

'Don't excite him, William.'

'No, ma'am. I won't, ma'am. Don't give me the strap, ma'am!' Having regained his cap, William flourished it, bowed elaborately. Henry giggled.

Sour as ever, as the cats' milk congealing in the row of saucers set out on the back porch, Ellen did not smile. She would be thirty-four now, William thought, a mere two years older than Henry, though she looked ten years his senior. Her brown and silver hair, scraped back and rolled over her ears, looked thin, old-fashioned. Fine lines had multiplied around her eyes and mouth.

'Father is inside.' Ellen stood back to let him pass. As he went by, with Henry close behind, William took one of her hands and gave it a clumsy squeeze. Ellen turned her cheek to him, as if she thought he might kiss her. When he didn't she was glad: he smelled rank.

'Perhaps you could wash before you go into him.' Her voice was quiet, cold. 'Have you no luggage?'

William shook his head.

'Henry will give you something. Dress in his room.' Ellen hurried him through the hall, gesturing quickly towards the front parlour as they passed its closed door.

From *Belief.*

Onehunga Bay

ROBERT SULLIVAN

The ripples on the bay are not from the wind. They
are from the traffic on the causeway. A stone perimeter
had once made this a brackish pool, but now the sand,
becoming shoal, swallows the sound of flying microlites.

Two women are wheeling their babies along the brackish beach
where the waves fling and curl the culvert weed – 'what a shitty
arse stink!' they shriek – revelling in the irony of babies
sound asleep, wrapped in nappies, that sort of disposable routine.

The weed on the bay is high today. The microlites' present height
ends by firing distress flares, adding to Daedalus' ancient special
f/x. First hesitate politely, then accept that the dog prints,
the shoe and jandal prints are very old. The local Borough Council

have opened a real turd-in-the-box. The splats of come
discovered on the causeway were spoor of Man O' War
that rose too high, then died before the turning tide.
A lone heron, with silvered scissor beak, is a hero

that snips and snaps an enemy stretch of seaweed, breaking
the length. Another new filter station resembles any hacienda:
Decrabond on brick. Its owners are rich: SWITCH OFF
   OZONE LIGHTS
BEFORE ENTERING WET WELL: but not enough to arrest
   the killer

vegetation. Our heroic heron signals and lifts from the shifting
swell, spurting buckets of clag just whiskers from the man.
An airport bus bursts in, recklessly rattling the causeway asphalt
to see with sleepy eyes three white spots jettisoned from

the precipice of a dead heron's feathertips. Repeating that,
I turn my Praktika, foci circling and shooting a series
of stones' thrown images, ripples beneath our setting eyelids.
Hard to imagine this was the launch pad for the great

Manukau fleets. Aa, tooia mai, te waka! Ki te urunga, te waka!
Ki te moenga, te waka! Ki te takotoranga i takoto ai – te waka!
Aa, haul the canoe to its rest, the canoe to its bed,
the canoe to the place where it will lie – te waka!

From *Jazz Waiata*.

At the Auckland Museum

DENIS BAKER

After a while we left the bench and the soccer game and went through the Museum, looking at artefacts from the Pacific and the permanent exhibitions of the wars in Europe that New Zealanders had died in, stopping to watch the Maori cultural show. At this I was a stranger too, as much a tourist as the Americans and the gaggle of Japanese language students also there, and was saddened by this. Yet at the same time in a strange way the performance resonated, reminded me of being in a place you called home, surrounded by a culture you couldn't fully identify with, feeling lost as a result.

We left the Museum and following the trails at the edge of the park through the native bush, emerged in Parnell where we had lunch at a restaurant with heavy white linen table cloths and surly wait-staff. We drank a nice bottle of riesling, ate seafood, had an argument, sulked and eventually made up on our way home. It was typical of our days together and while they might have failed to reunite us in the way Angela was hoping for, they did at least get us used to being in each other's company again.

I have to admit that to a greater extent, I enjoyed these days. By having a visitor and being placed into the role of knowledgeable local, I was forced to reacquaint myself with the city, to see its flaws and its beauty through new eyes. The more I saw the more I liked and through it Angela accidentally achieved what I'd failed to do since I'd been back. She put me in touch, showed me my place in the city, and at the end of it I belonged.

From *On a Distant Island*.

A Parnell encounter

FRANK SARGESON

It was late one fine summer afternoon when I walked slowly up to Wynyard Street carrying my suitcase, my head full of memories while my eyes noted all that had remained the same (the carved stone faces on the Supreme Court building, the tiny dome on the top of St Andrew's church steeple, the view across to Parnell); and those things that had changed so much that I had some difficulty in remembering. The trees in Government House grounds were not quite the same, nor were they on Constitutional Hill, and even the old house seemed to have shrunk in stature; but then I was taller myself and so were the trees in the street outside. There was, nevertheless, that which was so indefinably different about the house, that walking up the steps I was suddenly uncertain as it occurred to me to wonder who would open the door to me. Had my Uncle Hilary lived on there all alone, and did he still go out only of an evening? Did Edwina still keep house for him? And might she not say that my uncle was not at home, as I had heard her so often reply on my grandmother's behalf? After I had rung the housebell, I was looking at the painted-over places from which my grandfather's plate and bell had been removed, when the door was opened by a shortish, middle-aged, bald-headed man in a singlet and sailor's bell-bottomed trousers: he was drying his hands on a towel which was tucked round his waist to serve as an apron, and he asked me to excuse him as he was busy cooking. I asked to see my uncle, and he replied that I would have to travel a long way to pay a call on him. 'Mr Chelton's away in Blighty, mate,' he said. 'Or he might be sunning himself in the Canary Islands seeing what the weather's like in the old country at this time of the year.' I remained silent while he looked me up and down, and then he asked, 'You a friend of Mr Chelton's, mate?' I replied that I was his nephew, and he chuckled. 'Nephew? I never heard about him having a nephew, mate.' I stared back at him, puzzled to know what his thoughts might be, and having the word nepotism rolling around in my own, and then I informed him of my name and said that I had formerly lived in the house with my grandparents; but he yawned while he shook his head, and asked if I would mind excusing him or one of his pots might be boiling over. 'Is Pepper still alive?' I asked. 'Oh, come on in, mate,' he said. 'I don't get the strength of you, but you might be able to make your alley good with mister.' And he waved me into my grandmother's old room while he trotted on through to the kitchen.

The room was very little different. There was no sign of either Robinson or Marlowe, but Pepper could not be bothered to desist from trying to bite his way out of his cage when I spoke to him. Round the walls were the familiar books; and there was also my grandmother's German piano, with the delicate blue silk that showed behind its fretwork a little more faded now. Virtually the only difference was that the big table, on which I had always had to clear a space among my grandmother's painting things before I could do my lessons, had been replaced by a much smaller one which left space for some additional armchairs; and my sense of having returned home after a long absence was so strong that I closed my eyes the better to relish it: while I had them closed I lightly touched the piano keyboard, and was chagrined to discover that I was mistaken about the identity of the note I had sounded. It was while I was comforting myself with the thought that the piano was probably out of tune, that I heard myself greeted in the most resonant, most beautifully articulated and modulated voice which I had ever heard at close quarters. The owner of the voice was a tall man in middle age with a fine head of thick grey hair: he wore a plum-coloured velvet jacket and a shirt of pleated silk with a large bow tie. His manners were such as I had never encountered since the days when I lived in the house: that is to say, he was both casual and friendly, but I knew for a certainty that from the moment he entered the room he was observing every detail about myself, even though he did not allow it to appear that he was noticing anything at all. I introduced myself, and after telling me that his name was Morgan, John Morgan, he went on to say that on account of the war and shipping difficulties the date of my uncle's return from the old country was uncertain: in the meantime he had a lease of the house. 'Hilary,' he said, 'never mentioned any relatives.' He confessed, however, that they had known each other only a short time before the trip to England had been decided upon. 'I wrote my uncle a letter,' I said. 'From Hamilton.' 'Ah, recently,' he replied. 'Yes, I remember.' And he said that of course the letter had been forwarded on. 'I am sorry,' he said, 'that you have been disappointed in your expectations of seeing your uncle, but if you wish I can give you his accommodation address.' He was sitting at ease with his legs crossed and his fingertips touching, but it did not escape me that he was intimating he had covered all the ground and there was nothing more to say: I nevertheless had some difficulty in adjusting myself to the situation, even though I had the comfort of Ernie's so far untouched five-pound note in my pocket. I hesitated, and he inquired if it was a short visit I was paying to the city. I replied with some account of my school-teaching intentions, and went on to mention my problem of accommodation. 'Ah,' he said, and perhaps just a shade too readily to fit the perfection of his manners, 'I should like to be in a position to offer you that, but unfortunately we are quite a houseful.' And interpreting his words as my definite dismissal, I expressed my thanks to him as he accompanied me to the door. I was, however, very conscious of carrying with me the word 'we' out into the street; and as luck would have it, I had not gone twenty yards when I was enabled to guess who it might refer to, for I was recalled from the abstraction of my thoughts by the sight of two very slender, very elegantly-dressed young men who embarrassed me with their concentrated stare as I passed them. For my own part, I contrived to glance back in order to be certain about the house they entered: and I remember it was my final thought about my visit that although it was unlikely Mr Morgan would ever permit himself to be caught out in such a lapse from good manners, there were at least two people he knew who were not so particular.

From *Memoirs of a Peon*.

Bastion Point

SARAH QUIGLEY

April is cruel. Eliot said so. Everything is false – appearances, expectations. Every aspect of life is being swept towards some kind of ending, while instinct is crying, Stay, look back, only hard ground lies ahead. Yes, April is cruel, Eliot said so and now Claudia is about to prove it.

In Auckland April is more treacherous than in any other place. Days are warm as the wolf's breath, so that the bite of night is like a betrayal. The sun rocks slowly through the sky but the dark comes unexpectedly early. The trees turn gold and look radiant but hidden in the leaves the tuis croak of sadness.

Bastion Point. It has a safe sound to it but Haley feels more and more vulnerable as they drive in Claudia's car away from the city lights and up towards the sky. The threat seems to be felt only by her; Leith is unchanging as ever, and Claudia glitters and reflects off him. She is as luminous as Haley has ever seen her, and her talk devours the silence just as her car devours the dark miles.

Quasars are super-massive black holes that can swallow up whole stars

the energy surrounding them is brighter than a million billion suns

The gates are closed so they have to leave the car on the main road and walk up the hill. The obelisk stands above them like a tooth, and under it (Leith tells them) are the remains of the one-time prime minister Michael Joseph Savage.

—*Savage*, says Claudia, striding over the dark grass. —A good last name, couldn't be better if he'd invented it. What's your last name, Haley?

Haley trips over a clump of grass and Leith catches her, sets her on her feet.

—Careful! he says. —You're walking for two, remember.

Claudia's beautiful profile is as stony as the obelisk. She stalks ahead, leaving Leith, Haley and the boy-girl to follow. At the top, she sits in the moonlight and tries to start an argument with Leith about when the land was occupied by Maori protesters.

—It was 1978, she says definitely.

–I think it was 1977, says Leith, equably.

Haley knows little about it but she can feel dissidence in the very ground she is sitting on. She closes her eyes and hears hammering, sees rough wooden shacks; hears shouting, sees police batons falling.

Hears Claudia.

–Bloody English, she is saying. –Always marching into places that aren't their own, taking over.

–Claudia! says Leith, half-laughing, half-reproving. –Christ, you overstate things.

Haley can't even retaliate, is starting to feel that she will never have anything to say again. She hasn't felt this excluded from humanity since Bangkok airport, and God knows there have been some grim moments since then. She huddles down into her blanket, arranges it in a hood around her face with just enough space for breath. Still she doesn't feel secure, and the chill wind of Claudia's meanness makes her ears ache.

–D'you know what causes this meteor shower? asks Leith.

From *After Robert*.

Orakei

CHARLOTTE GRIMSHAW

Maria smoked a cigarette down by the mudflats, by the railway line. Bright light, photographic clarity. Gravel on the embankment sliding drily underfoot, blinding light arcing off the curving tracks. The turning tide sluiced water through the channel, the water flowed towards the estuary mouth. Sticks turned and turned on the surface, milky bubbles in the moving current rose up through the salt and floated swiftly away. By the railway line she smoked and watched, while the deep green water ran down to the sea. Seeing the sticks turn and turn, watching cars through the sunstrike creeping slowly up the saddle of the hill. Cars moving, water moving, wind over the water and nothing changed. Smoking and watching she saw it bitterly, that everything was beautiful, and nothing had changed.

By the railway station a car slowed and she heard yobbish hoots and lewd wolf-whistles, she glared at them smearily, how *could* they? As she walked back up to the cemetery gates a jogger swerved past and clipped her shoulder, she stared after him in dismay, how *could* he? Practically pushed her into the hedge, and the sharp sticks scratching her face. She swore at him weakly. *Fucking* joggers. He passed on with a swish of air and a waft of sweat and didn't look back. Great overdeveloped hams, tautly shuddering buttocks, legs pistoning away up the street. How could he? But why should he not? Why not?

She hurried on through the bland garden suburb, the indifferent streets. She caught the old man as he was driving his car through the cemetery gates.

'Sorry,' she said, getting in.

'It's OK.' He patted her knee. Then he squeezed her knee, relaxed his hand, squeezed it again. At the touch of his hand the hairs rose on the back of Maria's head. Her nose tickled. She raised her handkerchief to her face and looked at him – it was Leon's profile, the same features but thicker, heavier, more masculine. Leon grown heavy and male. The big fingers continued to flex on the scratchy nylon of her stocking and Maria suddenly entertained a vision of herself sprawled up against one of the broken graves, her pantyhose around her knees, the old man with the son's eyes fucking her to pieces on the surreal grass while the grey angels watched through mossy eyes and startled blackbirds rose over ruined bouquets and empty jars and blackened slabs.

But he turned his head and his eyes were weak and watery and not intent but hopeless, and the flexing of his hand was an involuntary wringing and nervous stroking, weak fluttering of an old man who was lost for words, who came to himself with a shake of his head and took his hand away and fumbled with the keys, accelerating the car forward with many muttered apologies and distracted sighs.

Shielding his eyes against the light, he turned out into the impossible blinder of the afternoon sun. Driving straight on into the west, the sun sunk low and burning, burning.

Golden light in the cemetery, yellow light on suburban rows. Weatherboards, neat hedges, rainbow sprinklers over the glowing grass. Maria rode with one hand on the dashboard, flinching when they stopped abruptly at red lights. Those Jews. In your village that time. Did you bury many? Were there many? Did you see? *I was a little boy. But the men worked hard all day.* Were there many? How could you bear it? How could life go on? *I was a little boy. There were twenty of them. Or thirty. Life went on. How could it not? How not…?*

They arrived at a brick house in Orakei. Leon's cousins

greeted them at the door. Don, a builder. Vaclav, a dentist. Aleta, plump mother of five wiry boys. All tall and amiable, long-nosed and blond. The old people gathered on the bright lawn, carefully enjoying the late afternoon sun, eating lemon cake, drinking coffee. Maria walked about the garden and the terrace, sat on a chaise longue on a concrete verandah and listened to the ugly-beautiful sounds of foreign languages: Czech, Polish, Yugoslav. She nodded and smiled, murmuring. Yes, I was the girlfriend. I'm the girlfriend. I was. Yes, I adored him. Yes.

An old lady on crutches tottered over and lowered herself down. She looked a hundred years old, dressed like a fortune-teller in heavy eyeliner, bright lipstick, a black scarf over her head tied tightly under her chin.

'I am aunty,' she whispered harshly, rolling her eyes to heaven and fastening claw-like hands on to Maria's arm. 'When he was this baby, I rock him on my knee…' She drew in a sharp, rattling breath and peered beadily sideways at Maria. 'You are the girlfriend?'

'Yes.'

The old lady nodded and sighed, closed her eyes, pressed her claws to her lacy breast. 'My dear, already you must have cried a thousand tears!'

'Oh yes, a thousand. *More!*' Desperate spray of cake crumbs, flapping of the unfurled hanky. In the reflection of the glass French door Maria glimpsed her own wooden and humiliated smile.

Nodding and blinking and sniffing exhilaratedly, as if a funeral were a stiff walk in the alps or a cold swim in the sea the old lady wiped tears from her own milky eyes, rose and crutch-walked efficiently away. Maria smoothed her hair automatically, silently consumed more lemon pie.

But I haven't cried, Maria thought. Not like that. It won't come. And I don't know how to. Maybe it's just – and forgive me if this sounds strange – maybe it's just because I'm so *afraid.*

From *Guilt.*

Walking Tamaki Drive

DENIS BAKER

Julie had a light jacket on and we were on Tamaki Drive taking Ana, her German short-haired pointer, for an evening walk along the waterfront. The tide was full and the sea reflected the glow of the streetlights. Ana pranced quietly along in front of us, her claws tacking audibly on the pavement, every so often swinging her head, checking we were keeping up. Her walk was a delicate sound, like clocks slightly out of unison. Occasionally she would accelerate a step or two to chase one of the sizeable cockroaches that lived in the sea wall and her beat would double.

'That's why she doesn't have a boyfriend,' said Julie. 'Because she's always working. And she works hard …'

'Because she doesn't … got it,' I said. 'One of those.'

'Sort of. I hate to pigeon-hole her. It hasn't been that easy for her – or that simple. The guy she was living with in London got scared and took off with some bimbo waitress. He'd been shagging her for ages apparently, 'just a thing', but then he split with her leaving Susan with the flat and mortgage. Not to mention a shattered heart. Some people are such pricks. It was all sweet for her, all the things she wanted: man, house, kids in the future and he just dumped her cold. Packed and left in a morning, said he wasn't ready for the responsibility or some fucking lame excuse. Since then there's been a couple of guys, Larry, another guy that looked promising, but she's gun-shy, majorly sensitive to being messed around.'

'I didn't realise.'

There was nothing in her voice to suggest she was saying all this for my benefit, or that she was reproving me in any way. We walked on towards Tamaki Yacht Club, the harbour lights blinking on our left. Julie took off her jacket and knotted it around her waist. It had been a long time since I'd walked around here at nine o'clock at night.

I yawned and Julie looked at me quizzically. I was working too hard and was tired at all the wrong times. 'Sorry.'

'Don't mean to keep you up,' she said.

A couple was walking towards us and as they approached Ana dropped back until she was only a couple of paces ahead of Julie. As they passed she didn't move or behave differently, just padded along, but once they were gone she moved out to the ten or so paces she'd had on us before. It was the second time I'd seen her do this.

'Well-trained dog.'

Julie laughed. 'Just protective. Plus I like walking alone. We do this quite a lot and she makes me feel safer.'

Growing up we'd had a border collie, keeping him until I was about fifteen. The day he was put to sleep we were at school and my father drove him to the vet's without telling my sister or me. Humane or not it was two days before I spoke to my father again and I don't think Mary ever forgave him.

'Susan had Ana's sister – we bought them together – but with the café and everything, she couldn't look after her. After a few weeks she gave her back. Got a house alarm instead.'

'Some friends had a dog in London,' I said. 'I thought it was the cruellest thing. Only a little park to play in. Stuck in a house with a smudge of a backyard.'

'Not fair,' she said. Ana glanced around as if in agreement.

At Mission Bay we stopped at one of the cafés choosing to sit outside, Ana tethered to my chair leg. Julie ordered a hot chocolate and I had a glass of wine, and the waiter, endearing himself to Julie, brought Ana a water bowl.

Thursday night and the café was nearly full. A constant stream of people wandered by the table dressed for an evening out.

'Occasionally as kids we used to come to the movies here,' I said. 'The Saturday matinee. There was a dairy here that sold the biggest ice creams, and a fruit and vege shop and a hardware store run by a man with a big grey moustache. Now there are just cafés and restaurants and hair salons.'

'Everything has changed,' she said.

'I think that's the hardest thing about being back. Not so much the physical change, but the ideas behind the change. I don't understand where they came from. Once you could buy things here, for your life, now it's a place to pass the time rather than somewhere to live.'

She smiled. 'Maybe you're just getting old and nostalgic.'

'Maybe. There just seems so little to hang on to. This seems so flimsy, such a façade.'

She fished around the rim of her cup with a teaspoon and salvaged a chocolate-sodden marshmallow. 'It is flimsy, it's new. But this isn't the whole country.'

'No, but the ideas everywhere have changed. And you can't grasp what you don't understand. I haven't been part of it.

Sometimes I think that it's not me, that it won't ever be me. I don't know who I am here.'

'We were all the same,' she said, 'ask Susan. It took her ages.'

'And you?'

'God, it took me years.' She smiled again. There were dark patches of dried chocolate in the corners of her mouth. 'It's worse if you don't decide, if you drift. It doesn't matter where you are then. You can't be in one place by default thinking maybe you'll go somewhere else, because then you're not anywhere.'

'That's why you thought the job was a good idea.'

'Mostly. You needed an interest, some kind of anchor.'

'An anchor or a chain?'

She smiled. 'You choose, but it's kinda hard to have one without the other.'

After we'd finished our drinks we took Ana onto the beach where Julie tried to exhaust her. It was useless. There was hardly anyone about and she tore up and down the beach ignoring everyone but Julie and occasionally myself, turning tight circles and bulleting past us.

'I'm going to take her to Tokaanu next time. She'll love it.'

'We used to throw sticks into the Waitahanui for Charlie so he'd have to swim back upstream to return them. Good exercise.'

'I bet,' she said. 'Ana would like that.'

'When he got older he got wise and would swim to the side, climb out, then run the sticks back to us. Little beggar.'

Ana came bounding back and Julie cupped her head, talking to her in a silly dog voice, scratching her behind the ears before sending her off again.

We sat down on the sand and shells and presently Ana returned with a stick she'd found, dropping it next to me, then moving away a short distance.

'She likes you,' said Julie.

'Me and dogs, we have a common bond.'

'Really?'

'Oh yes. Lots of women have called me a dog.'

She laughed. 'From what I know of your relationship history, I don't believe it.'

She drew her knees up under her chin and ran her hands through the sand. I threw the stick as far as I could sitting down.

Ana was good, undemanding, dropping the stick and waiting patiently, taking her time sniffing around before bringing it back. I lit a cigarette and offered Julie one.

'Thank you,' she said. The non-smoker at rest.

Behind us Mission Bay was brightly lit and the shadows

from the pohutukawas between us and the beachside restaurants, blanketed us. She was thirty-five, a little freckled, green-eyed with gentle brown eyebrows and short brown hair. She was understanding and kind. Yet both she and Susan were alone.

'Can I ask you a question?'

She rolled eyes. 'We know what that means. God, go on, if you must.'

'You and Larry? You never, you know ... got together? You just seem, I don't know, quite well suited.'

She laughed loudly. 'Larry? No. I mean ... just no. It's not like that. You know about him and Susan ... They were close. We're close too, but it's more familial than anything.' She chuckled again. 'No.'

'I see.' It was quiet on the beach, the trees and distance blocking out most of the noise of the few cars on the road behind us, just the waves sloughing off the sand. Ana came back and I threw the stick again. 'Because of Susan. Does that make a difference?'

She looked up. 'No,' she said, 'not at all.'

I held her eye and leant across and kissed her. My heart was thumping like a sixteen-year-old's, but she didn't move. Instead she closed her eyes as our lips touched. I pushed closer and she put her palm on my chest, breaking the contact.

'No,' she whispered.

'But ...'

'It's not ... it's not what you want, Paul.'

There was nothing in her voice beyond a statement of fact. I sat back to protest, but nothing came out. I had no argument. It had been the briefest press of lips. I should have felt embarrassed, but I wasn't, just disappointed. Out in the harbour a boat was making its way back to land, visible only by its navigation lights, the white in the bow, the red like an eye showing the port side.

'Dog,' she said, looking at me before I could speak again.

'What?'

'Where's that bloody dog?' she said with a grin, and jumped up, brushing the sand off her bum. She whistled once, loud and arching, and in seconds Ana appeared sprinting out of the shadows low across the beach like a missile again, racing up to us, her tongue lolling as if laughing at me.

From *On a Distant Island.*

Ode to Auckland

James K. Baxter

Auckland, even when I am well stoned
On a tab of LSD or on Indian grass
You still look to me like an elephant's arsehole
Surrounded with blue-black haemorrhoids.

The sound of the opening and shutting of bankbooks,
The thudding of refrigerator doors.
The ripsaw voices of Glen Eden mothers yelling at their children,
The chugging noise of masturbation from the bedrooms of the
    bourgeoisie,
The voices of dead teachers droning in dead classrooms,
The TV voice of Mr Muldoon,
The farting noise of the trucks that grind their way down Queen
    Street
Has drowned forever the song of Tangaroa on a thousand
    beaches,

The sound of the wind among the green volcanoes,
And the whisper of the human heart.

Extract, *Collected Poems.*

Jogging the Viaduct Basin

WITI IHIMAERA

So on with the jogging shorts and out.

I alternate my mornings between gym and jogging. This morning the first ten minutes of jogging are absolute agony. Everything refuses to move in unison. My lungs are saying, No. My legs are saying, Ouch. My chest is asking, Do we have to? My head keeps on asserting the physical benefits to them all, even if grimly.

From the flat my usual course is triangular. Along the main road to the suburban shopping centre. Then cut through the traffic, through the woods past the athletic park and The Teps. Finally, back via the motorway to the bridge, up the viaduct and the main road home again. Today I duck through the morning traffic and sprint to catch the lights at the intersection. The adrenalin of beating the lights makes my heart pump.

Then, coming in the opposite direction I see the familiar figure of Italian Stallion. It was at a party at his place that I met Chris.

'Go, David, go,' he yells.

He has shining brilliantine hair and laughs as I take up his challenge. Across and against the lights, the traffic already moving, weaving this way and that like an American gridiron player. Fend off a player here. Into the gap there.

Car horns burp, outraged, and brakes squeal.

Touchdown.

'Way to go!' Italian Stallion laughs.

His running partner, Now You See It Now You Don't, catches up with him. He offers tantalising glimpses as he lopes along. He and Italian Stallion have been together for eight years now. After such a long time together they have become joined at the hip. Although true love has never run smooth, they have proven that by triumph of tenacity and will, male to male relationships can, and do, last.

By the time I reach the third side of my triangle my blood is singing and my breath steams in the air. On mornings like this the world is re-created in all its innocence.

Two elderly Asian women are performing Tai Chi movements in the park, slow-motion beauty in the dappling sun.

Then, zooming from The Teps and an early-morning swim, is The Noble Savage. Today not a flower in his ear but a piece of lustrous green jade. His car is filled with four young Maori boys and two women.

'Kia ora, David.'

As always, my heart leaps to see him. His is a new gay tribe working to uplift the causes of all Maori and Polynesian homosexuals, bisexuals, transvestites and lesbians. They are chanting as they come forward through their own homophobic world as well as ours. They are saying to us all, gay and straight:

Move over. We're coming through.

From *Nights in the Gardens of Spain.*

Parnell and the Auckland Art Gallery

Diane Brown

~ beware of red dresses ~

'A cocktail party? But I've got nothing to wear,' cries Moppy.

'Please, allow me to buy you something.'

'You can't. Can you?'

'Of course. Who else do I have to spend money on? And it pleases me so much to see you dressed up.'

Vincent insists they go to Parnell. These days Moppy shops in malls, though she wonders if she is getting too old to wear mass-produced clothes. The Parnell shop is full of muted colours and fabrics that swing even on the hanger. If further evidence is required of the exclusiveness of the clothes, observe the tones in the shopkeeper's voice.

'Are you looking for anything in particular, Madam?' There is a slight nuance of confusion beneath the confidence. She is not quite sure where to place this couple in her marbled interior. Not tourists, or Remuerites.

'What do you think of this, Vincent?' Moppy holds up a black crepe dress with all the attention paid to the low-scooped back. She secretly loves her unblemished back. 'Strong,' one long-ago lover called it.

'No, too long. I prefer this.' He holds up a skimpy bright red dress. The material has a slight sheen to it, the arms are cut away. It is short and straight.

'Don't you think it's a bit small?'

'No. Try it on.'

Moppy does what she is told. The dress does surprising things for her imperfections, skimming over her waist and stopping short to reveal her legs. Moppy pinches her upper arms. She regrets the slight invasion of flabbiness.

'Wow.'

It is not the dress Moppy would have chosen for herself. Not a dress you could wear to a film festival or to a café, but …

She averts her eyes as Vincent pays. In its expensive brown paper bag the dress is heavier than expected.

'How does it feel to be a kept woman?' asks Jill when Moppy brings it around for inspection.

'That's a bit cutting, isn't it? Why can't I have some small pleasures? Aren't you the one who lives in a seaside mansion?'

'You know perfectly well it wasn't my choice to build such an extravagant house. Anyway, Robert and I are married. I'm just worried that you're getting in too deep. You know what you're like: you get to the stage where you can't extract yourself. It was the same with Tim. And Vincent's not right for you. He's too dependent.'

It's true. Moppy is getting tired of Vincent's constant phone calls, morning and night, as if he can't breathe without her.

～ the arty cocktail party ～

The cocktail party is in the Art Gallery. Vincent's firm is entertaining clients. A private showing of photographs. No one is all that interested in looking at the walls. Guests are there to partake of the sauvignon blanc and the morsels of food and flattery.

Vincent clutches Moppy's arm.

'I'm so proud of you. You look so beautiful in my red dress.'

'Does this mean you want it back? I could take it off. Now if you like.' She starts to unzip the back.

'Don't be silly. This is business. Anyway it's yours.'

He steers Moppy in the direction of a man she would describe as a hunk. Tall, dark curly hair greying at the temples.

'Moppy, this is Rodney Spence.' Rodney's wearing a thinish grey silk suit which seems to flow from his shoulders.

'Delighted to meet you, Moppy,' says Rodney. 'Vincent's told me all about you.'

'But not me about you. What do you do?' asks Moppy.

Rodney holds a piece of polenta topped with red pepper delicately between his fingers. 'Architect.'

'Oh, you did Robert Fisher's house.'

'Indeed. Friend of yours?'

'Mm. Well Jill is.'

'And what do you think of their house?'

'Stunning. But not for me. I prefer to live in a bach. Which is just as well as I don't have any money.'

'What do you do?' His voice is polite and without curiosity.

'I'm a mother, a tutor, a sales assistant, an ex-wife.'

'And lover,' Vincent interjects. It's the first time Moppy has known him to be so assertive.

'And artist when I get the time.'

'Another one. The world's full of wannabes.'

'Of course, but it's true.'

'It comes down to priorities. Obviously being an artist is not so important to you. Anyway, stick with Vincent, he's crazy about you.'

'Talk about arrogant.' Moppy hisses to Vincent when Rodney sidles off. 'And I didn't notice you defending me. All you did was claim me as your lover.'

'Well it's true, isn't it? Although one day I'd like to be more.'

They concentrate on the photographs. The light falling on male flanks reminds Moppy of a McCahon. Her favourite.

'I've got some nude photos of myself, you know,' she says to Vincent.

'Really? Can I see them?'

'Of course. I was at my peak. Nineteen and without drooping breasts.'

From *if the tongue fits*.

Speeding down Queen Street

Tina Shaw

The last time she'd seen Oliver they were on their bikes and speeding down Queen Street – at a time, pre-mountain bikes, pre-bike helmets even, when hardly anybody cycled around the city. *Country hiiicks,* sang Clare, as the wind rushed at her face and reddened her ears, and she'd never felt more alive, weaving in and out among the traffic. Coming down the higher part of the hill that was Queen Street past Myers Park, Oliver was up ahead, hunched into the wind, and she was coming down fast behind him; then, without warning, a person stepped out in front of her.

She screamed, braked, knocked into the person, and went over the handlebars.

'I'm sorry, so sorry,' she gasped, getting up, glancing over herself: no scrapes on knees, no broken limbs, no cuts even, astounding – and to be confronted with a boy/man, sorter than herself but with a browned face which had a hint of the wizened about it. He was dressed in sagging dirty jeans and some kind of black sweatshirt; his hair was matted and black; his fingernails (she noticed later as he picked up her bike for her) were dirty. Some kind of a street kid/man? They were a problem for police in the city, and Clare noticed that the tumble had happened right outside Myers Park, where street kids liked to sleep. And Oliver was slowly struggling back up the hill. Clare couldn't help thinking of the scene in Beckett's novel about the girl getting knocked by a car and the loaf of bread she'd been carrying making a slow arc through the air. All of this noted in a portion of a second.

'God, I'm sorry, are you all right?' Clare, distraught, became even thinner and whiter.

The boy/man just grinned, and folded her in his arms, hugging her tightly. Then he retrieved her bike from its louche angle on the street, and handed it back to her.

Oliver came up as the boy/man wandered off. 'I thought you'd killed that guy.' And Clare, giggling, said, 'So had I.'

'He could've got hurt, the idiot, just stepping out like that.'

'He hugged me,' sniffed Clare, remounting her bicycle, though continuing down the hill more sedately.

From *City of Reeds*.

Outside Smith & Caughey's

Tina Shaw

Oliver happened to run into Lou outside Smith & Caughey's one afternoon. He wouldn't have recognised her – she looked quite different, her lips hard and sharp with red lipstick (she could have been wearing a mask), and there was something odd about her clothes – except that she had glanced into his passing face and he had thought she was Clare. He had been about to call out when he realised his mistake in time.

'Lou,' he cried. 'How's it going?'

'Fine.' She smiled falsely, and Oliver's old altruistic instincts were aroused. It seemed like a long time since he'd heard anything about Lou.

'Want a coffee? I'm buying.'

They sat in a coffee bar. Louise had dropped out of university and was living on the dole. She'd also been kicked out of her flat, though she wouldn't say why – just that they were a pack of wankers – and she was dossing down on a friend's couch until she found somewhere to stay.

'Y'know, Oliver,' Louise muttered, hands around her cup. 'You seem older, somehow.'

Oliver pulled back his shoulders unconsciously. 'Well, I suppose it happens to the best of us. Gotta grow up sometime, eh.'

Lou started to light a cigarette, but the match slipped from between her fingers. Oliver leaned over and did it for her, the flame flaring between them for a moment. She looked at him then, and she was the old Louise, full of bravado. 'So what d'you do for fun, Oliver?'

'Ah, well.' He frowned, trying to think. 'Not very much, I don't suppose. Clare and I go to the pictures sometimes, when she's got time. She swots a lot.'

Lou nodded sagely. 'That's a problem I don't have any more.'

When they left the coffee bar, she led him into an empty alleyway between grey blank-walled buildings. She pressed him against a wall, and got her hand down his pants. 'Lou,' he gasped, 'I –' She kissed him with an emotion much baser than lust, the lipstick smearing, silencing any protests. Grabbing up her skirt in fisted bunches, she pushed him inside her with fury, while Oliver could only cry out, paralysed against the wall which was scraping his back, his thin shoulder blades grazing against the bricks; and it didn't seem very long before Lou was crying, her face wet and salty, slicked sheen, and she was sobbing against his best seersucker tie like the world had come to an end.

'… Lou?'

As if remembering where she was, she took a deep breath and extricated herself, straightening her face and her clothes. A little flip-top mirror came out of her bag and the lipstick was repaired, the cheeks patted with powder.

'Thank you, Oliver,' she said primly, 'I needed that.' She looked up at the looming facades around them, as if pondering something quite deep. Though what she was really thinking was how it was time she started earning some decent money. Money, thought Louise, could save and protect you. 'In fact, I think I'll be quite all right, now.' She started to walk away.

'Er, Lou –?'

She turned back with raised eyebrows. Oliver was just as gawky as ever.

'That was phenomenal. When can I see you again?'

From *City of Reeds*.

Who is reading poetry in 2021?

ANNA JACKSON

Hems are up again. In a short
yellow shift dress she sits
in the middle of Queen street
under the giant Russian sunflowers,
her legs crossed to conceal
her crotch, her ankles aching
just a bit.

She is my second-to-last reader.
She holds one of the few copies
left of my collected verse,
hoping someone will notice
her choice.

She nurses her gin for as long
as she can, but she will leave

before it gets dark.
It will take her an hour
to walk home through the park.
From Dunedin to Auckland
without stopping, those
were the days, when
you could get in your car
and drive!

My second-to-last reader
would have liked to have lived
in 1991.

Her father won't let her play
his Bic Runga CD anymore,
but she sings the words herself
as she walks under the sunflowers
of Queen st, through the wildflowers
of K Road, brushing brambles
aside as she heads over
the Bond st bridge.

Her skin is scribbled over
with scratches and welts
from the weeds,
but the poetry of the past
is in her head and driving her out
of her skin, bursting through, bursting
through to the wild days of 1991
when we could get in our cars
and drive.

Karangahape Road

PAULA MORRIS

Karangahape Road smelled.

Once upon a time it stank of heavy, sickly incense swung by a writhing procession of Hare Krishnas, turning the footpath ice-block orange outside Rendells and George Court's every Thursday night. Virginia remembered the sight and smell of them perfectly, along with the tinny, tinsel sound of their tambourines. That was the only time the Setons went walkabout on K Road: Thursday nights, before they abandoned it altogether for Friday nights at Lynn Mall, past Waikumete cemetery, just ten minutes drive from home.

Later, when she was a teenager, the odour became more subtle and greasy, fried food from takeaway bars wafting through the open car windows, speeding past the Pink Pussycat on the way home from occasional strained family outings to see musicals at the Mercury. And the Mercury itself had its own scent – audience smells of sweat and powder, freshly applied lipstick and melting ice-cream, part of the indelible aroma of her adolescence.

There was still a touch of chip- and kebab-fuelled grease about the street, and traces of incense, too, lingering in the acoustic-tiled India Emporium. But it was traffic and coffee you could smell up and down the length of the road – not as long as it once seemed, elbowing Grafton and Grey Lynn out of the way, but really just four bridged blocks.

It was Sunday morning, and Virginia had driven in with her father to see Rob's new place and meet the elusive Lia, who looked, as it turned out, neither Chinese nor Samoan.

'If you ask me, she looks about fourteen,' muttered Jim, peering obediently into the hot-water cupboard during the tour of each of the apartment's slight rooms and narrow closets. The ninth-floor apartment was hermetically sealed, pale and still and new inside, like a suite in a hotel.

'So pleased to meet you, Ginny,' said Lia, squeezing Virginia's arm. She was an olive-skinned waif, not even half Rob's height, Virginia thought, despite her spiked hair and thick-soled shoes. She peered up at Virginia, intent and curious, as though she couldn't quite make out the family resemblance. 'Has Rob shown you the terrace?'

'I thought it was a fire escape,' said Jim, and Virginia nudged him.

'Jinx, did you see the tukutuku panel?' asked Rob. 'And the koru tiles in the bathroom? We like to buy Maori art and design.'

'And Samoan,' added Lia, glancing sideways at Rob. 'You have to be careful, you know,' she told Virginia. 'If you're buying tapa cloth to take back with you. There's a big difference between Tongan and Samoan.'

'Fijian,' said Rob.

'People don't realise,' said Lia, her voice bright.

Jim asked if anyone was planning to put the kettle on, but after some cajoling from Lia he agreed to go out to a café. They strolled back along K Road to St Kevin's Arcade (bit scruffy, Jim told Leeander when she got home) and turned their chairs to face the giant palm trees of Myers Park.

Virginia watched her father sipping frothy coffee from a white bowl, bobbing his head in and out like a child dunking for apples, oblivious to the splashes on his face. He was telling Lia about catching the tram to school along Karangahape Road and down Queen Street, past the park. Lia stared back at him with a slight frown, nodding, her teaspoon suspended in the air.

'Do they still have the lift in George Court's?' said Jim.

'I remember that,' said Virginia. 'The lift attendant would slam the cage doors shut and announce each floor. Not that there were many floors to go to.'

'It was really something, that lift,' said Jim. 'It went right up the centre of the shop.'

'They're apartments now, Dad,' Rob said impatiently. 'There was an article about one of them in *New Zealand House & Garden*; doesn't Leeander get that? The lift's gone. Security reasons.'

'That's right. I did hear they were turning the place into flats.'

'Apartments,' said Rob.

'I drive this way sometimes, you see,' Jim said to Lia. 'If I'm getting onto the motorway at Newton. I know they're doing some of this up, but it still looks a bit tatty to me.'

'You know, there are a lot of important and historic buildings in Auckland,' said Lia, nodding at them, frowning for emphasis. Something about Lia's manner irritated Virginia; she was treating Jim like an old man and Virginia like a tourist. 'That café we walked past on the way here, Brazil. You should go in there sometime. It has a vaulted ceiling, you know. It used to be the entrance to the Mercury Theatre.'

'Café now, is it?' said Jim. He lowered his latte bowl; it

185

clanged onto the saucer. 'Used to be a fruit shop, and once upon a time it was the entrance to the Prince Edward, long before it became the Mercury. First custom-built picture theatre in New Zealand, you know.'

'Did you go there, Dad?'

'Quite a bit, to the movies. Crowds of people cramming into that narrow entranceway. Couldn't be more than twelve feet wide.'

'You never said anything about it before, all those times we went to the Mercury,' said Virginia.

'All those bloody musicals,' said Rob. He raised his eyebrows at Lia.

'Nobody asked me,' said Jim, gazing out at the palm tree. 'Never came up. And anyway, nobody used to think of those places as historic then. They were just out-of-date, old-fashioned. It's lucky the Prince Edward didn't go the way of the Regent and get pulled down. Remember the Regent?'

'Just,' said Virginia.

Rob and Lia shook their heads.

'A lot of changes,' said Jim, looking down.

'You should come into the city on a weekend more often, Mr Seton,' said Lia.

'Call him Jim,' said Rob, climbing to his feet. 'I think I'll get something to eat. Anyone else? Jinx? Dad? Want to split a panini?'

'No thanks,' said Jim. He gulped the last of his coffee. 'You know, Lia, there used to be a nice little tea room-type place at the top of Rendells. Not a panini in sight, in those days. Though you know what they say: one man's panini is another man's filled roll.'

Lia gave Jim a long, tight-lipped smile as though, Virginia thought, he was not only old but quite possibly mentally ill.

From *Queen of Beauty*.

A night at the Balcony

CHARLOTTE GRIMSHAW

We roar out of the driveway taking a large piece of the foliage with us. Cracker leans out the window and tears leaves and branches from the windscreen while I cry with laughter in the passenger seat, already drunk enough to die laughing in a blazing auto wreck, every outrageous driving manoeuvre by Bernard sending me into greater merriment as I cling to the headrest of his seat. We head for the Balcony, Auckland's most fashionable all-hours bar. We head there at an indecently fast rate. We are flattened in our seats by the speed. We arrive in the carpark, the car festooned with flora and reeking of burning rubber.

Balcony is a crowded bar with wooden floors and a large balcony shaded partly by the roof of the building and partly by two willow trees which fall over the deck like stage curtains and filter the sunlight. During the day the bar is filled with rainy green light and at night it is lit with small lights hung from the trees. On most nights the place is full of the wealthy and significant people of Auckland, and many rich bachelors, and young hopefuls for Bernard to interview. Many beautiful and famous Auckland relationships have been formed at the bar.

Before I discovered the Balcony, before I met Stuart, my flatmates and I spent long and fraught evenings in a mean dive called the DB Waitemata in Central Auckland, where the poor and tattooed drinkers would grind their cigarette butts into the carpet, hurl jugs at one another and sometimes give one of us a really good beating in the toilets. One false move, any breach of etiquette and you could find yourself facing a Maori kangaroo court in the Ladies. Or, on lenient evenings you might just find yourself pushed out into the rain with a kick in the pants and a heavy jug whistling past your ears. It was the gun fanatic who insisted on going to the Waitemata instead of one of the more twee pubs, principally because he liked the violence and the filth, the meanness of it all. And he was the one who was never threatened. The headbanging Westies and sweating Samoans, the toothless, scarred, jailbird Maoris never gave him a minute of trouble. They could tell that he wanted it, they could tell that he would never run away.

Bernard and I fight our way to a table near the bar. Then Bernard takes his drink and makes his way around the tables, and

I drink wine and scan the room, happily drunk, pleased to be out of the house. The crime files weigh on me sometimes, especially after dark when the house is empty and the rooms are silent. The endless grime, the blood and the guts. I beam over at the people at the next table, admiring their cosmetic tans and their healthy *nouveau* wealth. How far removed they are from the blasted drunks in the DB Waitemata. And how different from all those accuseds in all those files who try to control their trembling hands, who stare with blank seagull eyes and mutter and sob and mumble and shout all their jumbled accounts of violence and misery and loss.

'Let's dance!' roars Bernard, and so we do.

Then we get back into the drinking. Bernard can really put it away, Bernard is a serious drinker, boozer and raver. By this time I am beginning to float and drift, the room has an unreal quality. Things are shifting and blurring. Time has gone slack, colours are pale. In the pastel-coloured Ladies as I am putting on makeup my balance goes and I fall against my own image, the rivers and tributaries of blood in my eyeball, the creases under the lower lids, beads of sweat and hairs and gaps in the makeup, all that terrible detail, up close. Shocked, I lever myself away, into focus. Shaking myself I carry out repairs, rubbing over smudges and filling in holes while behind me a young woman has locked herself into a cubicle and is unable to let herself out. A burly waiter is summoned and tries to talk her through the process of unlocking the door. She replies faintly and tearfully. Every few minutes there is a crash as she falls to the floor of the cubicle. 'I caaan't!' she wails. More waiters arrive and confer. They will have to break down the door. Reeling around at the mirror I notice a greasy imprint of my face on the glass, one kohl eye, one tan cheek, half a mouth, open, gasping.

'There's many a slip twixt cup and lip,' Bernard observes, pouring more all round. 'There's many a PRI to be suffered in such an establishment as we currently frequent. Make no mistake. Make no beg pardons. Drink?'

Bernard carries the scars of many a Piss Related Injury. Once he fell off a table and broke his ankle. Once he drove into a birdbath in the Auckland Domain, knocking himself out and killing a family of ornamental gnomes.

Stuart has developed a clever tactic when it comes to drinking and driving. It's this: Whenever he and I get drunk he makes me drive. 'Shit, darl,' he says patiently, 'I can't drive, I'm a criminal lawyer. You drive and I'll defend!'

At 4 a.m. Bernard volunteers to drive me back to Stuart's.

Cheerfully suicidal, I accept. We gather up all the phone numbers he has collected on slips of paper and menus and make for the carpark. We locate Bernard's car, parked lopsidedly, back wheels up on a concrete kerb, a branch of Stuart's pear tree still stuck across its roof. 'Look there are buds on it,' Bernard says. 'It must be spring.'

From *Provocation.*

Message from Mangere

A young pohutukawa blocks my view of our mountain now. In
    the darkness
below its slopes the ripples are eclectic: some from shoes thrown
by a lover who sang she was 'two steps on the water', others
                                 from the pull
of a full moon. The street lights flicker, electric flares
reflecting celestial gigawatts: from the mountain top you feel
    like God
looking on the galaxy that is Mangere. My civilization spreads
six billion miles, where Pioneer-X signals its existence. I accept
                          the emptiness,
the huge distances between the lines of the message: it may as well
broadcast here. And what about Mangere? the 'lazy' volcano,
    quarried for its scoria,
renowned for significant suburban wildlife: punks, streetkids, rastas,

heavy metal, Ronald McDonald is headmaster of the local primary
(it's true!).
Three kids piss in the doorway of their state house, each betting
on the speed of his stream as they drunk stumble from a concrete
ramp – prelude to lives
spent at Ellerslie? These infants of the very poor are far from
'unkillable', as Ezra Thump and the filthy rich would have us
believe.

Kenny and Dolly
sang it: Islands in the stream, that is what we are. Gee whiz,
my most urgent personal question is cash or cheque? In Mangere
the PM's the MP:
everyone and everything's in an inverse universe: you get karanga'd
on the shopping malls, the tangata whenua live in genuine
chipboard whares
overlooking the beautiful hei-tiki-shaped sewerage system,
the streetkids pop smack, listen to Grandmaster Flash, rap Michael
Jackson's BAD LP:
I'm Bad, shimon you know it, and of course they sleep in the
public
dunnies with the hole in the cubicle to prick your dick through.
Yeah Columbus

discovered Mangere, but meaty chicken breasts in sesame seed
        burger
ads are really insensitive: it's just the way, aha aha, you like it?
                                            No wonder
they spraybombed KILL A WHITE on the local Kentucky Fried.

From *Jazz Waiata*.

Shopping at St Luke's

PAULA MORRIS

People always said they looked alike, Virginia Seton and Tania French. Their grandmothers were sisters, and both the grand-daughters had the look of the eldest Grey girls about them – something to do with their mouths, their eyes, the way they held themselves. But Tania's skin was darker (I'm more Maori than you, she used to tell Virginia, back in the 'Mystery Date' days) and nowadays she seemed older than Virginia rather than a year younger – more grown-up, Virginia thought – because she had a daughter, Lily, who was nearly eleven.

'And a right madam she is too,' said Tania 'Nearly as tall as me and twice as cheeky as I was at her age. Precocious doesn't begin to describe it. She's really gutted about not being invited to the wedding – had her outfit all picked out. You know: clogs, knickers, necklace, the lot. So, where shall we start? This list is as long as the phone book.'

They'd met up in Mt Eden, at the Julia-approved

kitchenware store, its white walls stacked high with shining aluminium and crystal and enamel. Tania had been there before, she said, just looking; she'd been impressed most of all by the shopping bags, grey with white-ribbon handles, which seemed unnecessarily chic for pots and pans.

'But perhaps I've been coarsened,' she muttered to Virginia, 'by too many visits to Pak 'N Save.'

'A lot of it must be taken already,' said Virginia, staring down at the computer printout she'd been handed at the counter. 'How about glassware? Or china?'

'How about something cheap?'

'First floor.'

They trooped past display cases of Czech champagne flutes and English crockery, and scampered up the staircase. From the back, Tania looked like a schoolgirl, Virginia thought; she was still lithe and athletic in her skinny T-shirt and cropped jeans, a long dark plait of hair swinging between her shoulder blades, the heels of her mules clicking on each of the stairs.

'It's like the United Nations in here,' said Tania. 'Italian coffee machines, French frying pans. The tea towels are probably from the Phillipines.'

'There must be a kauri cheese board or two somewhere,' said

Virginia, looking around the room. 'Not on Julia's list, though. How about the sushi platter and carved chopstick set?'

'Very Pacific Rim of her,' said Tania.

'They're really into Japanese takeaways, Nick was telling me.'

'Speaking of Asians,' said Tania. She lifted an olive oil decanter, rolled her eyes at the price and placed it back on the shelf. 'My auntie Sue – you know, my Mum's sister – she was at my Mum and Dad's last weekend. I dropped Lily off there because I needed to go to St Luke's to get some of her Christmas presents before the place goes completely wild. She wants some lip gloss stuff and this feather boa collar thing – basically, she likes anything that makes her look like a trashy pop star. Anyway, when my auntie heard I was going to St Luke's, you know what she said? "Watch out for the Asians." I didn't understand what she meant at first. I thought she was warning me to mind my handbag. So I said to her: "What, are there Asian gangs marauding the shopping centres of Auckland? Should I keep an eye out for pickpockets?" And she gave me a funny look, like I was soft in the head, and said: "No. Just Asians".'

'And you should just watch out for them?' asked Virginia, and they both laughed.

'Exactly. Basically, they're not to be trusted,' said Tania, picking up a pepper grinder in each hand and tipping them upside down. 'Asians are the new Polynesians, but worse. That's what people think. You know, at least the Polynesians are sort of like Maoris. Brown and affable and overweight. They like playing cricket and rugby, picnics at the beach, that kind of thing. But Asians – they're completely alien. Who knows what they're up to.'

'Collecting shellfish out of season, you mean?'

'Yes, but even more dire than that: driving expensive cars, buying houses in Remuera, filling up private schools, taking all the places at university.'

'Ah, I see. *Rich* Polynesians.'

'With poor driving skills, no interest in assimilating, and bags of money. It's the post-colonial nightmare.'

'At least they're injecting money into the economy,' said Virginia. 'Isn't that a good thing?'

'Not to mention opening lots of really great Asian restaurants and markets,' said Tania.

Virginia checked the list for the next group of items. 'You want to look at tablecloths, place-mats and napkins?'

'If you think I could get away with it. You know, I bet Julia calls them napkins, too. She's such a snob, your sister.'

'We all are,' said Virginia. 'You don't have to get her anything if you don't want to. She probably won't notice. They've had a truckload of stuff from Nick's side of the family already. One of his uncles gave them a washing machine.'

'Oh, she'll notice all right,' said Tania. 'Actually, I think I've decided. I'm going to go for the pestle and mortar. Or is it a mortar and pestle? Anyway, it's the perfect gift for Julia. It costs more than it should, she'll hardly ever use it, and it's symbolic of how she's ground us down over the years.'

'She's not that bad,' said Virginia, laughing.

'You've always been a softie.'

'She's the only sister I've got. Well, except for Alice.'

'Have one of mine,' said Tania. 'One's in France, thinking she's hot shit, and the other one's in Auckland, thinking – well, she thinks she's hot shit too, actually.'

'Come on, we have to pay downstairs. And then let's go for a coffee.'

Tania picked up the pestle and mortar and sniffed inside the bowl. 'What are you buying, by the way?'

'One of those copper-based pans, I think. I want to get Julia something that'll last for ever. Something she can't break, or throw away by accident.'

'Something she can hit Nick over the head with,' said Tania, following Virginia down the staircase. 'Nothing lasts for ever, by the way.' She raised her voice. 'Not even nuclear waste or Tupperware. Hey Gin, if you don't want it, can I have the bag?'

A shop assistant in a blue-striped apron stopped what she was doing (packing a Villeroy and Boch sugar bowl in an elegant grey gift box) and gave them both a long, cold look.

From *Queen of Beauty*.

The bird

Albert Wendt

Iona visits his grandparents, Faga and Maopo, at 11 am every Monday, when Malia, his oldest sister, and her husband and their three children who live with their grandparents are at work and school, because he wants his grandparents to himself for the one-hour duration of his visit. Iona says nothing to Sam, his cousin, who is driving them to his grandparents' in Mangere.

Hot summer day. No wind. He loves the heat. When he gazes out at the Manukau, the dazzling morning light ricocheting off the surface of the black water cuts into the core of his eyes and he has to look away.

No one about in the street. Sam stops the car in front of Number 134. Iona gets out and, pausing at the front gate, concludes once again that their family home is the most expensive one in the street. He'd wanted to buy them a larger house outside South Auckland but they'd refused, insisting they wanted to finish their lives in the modest state house they'd raised him and his sisters in. Besides, their church, closest aiga and friends were there. So he'd bought the house, gutted and renovated it completely, thrown out all the old furniture and appliances and refurnished it with what Faga told her friends at church was 'the most expensive furniture and things this side of Heaven'. He always gives his grandparents the best. After all, they'd struggled in shit factories and shit cleaning jobs to raise him, his two sisters and cousins, after their parents had died in that horrific car crash, when his dad had been bloody drunk, full to his violent gills! Yes, for over twenty years Faga and Maopo had slaved their guts out for them.

He pushes open the gate and is immediately in a sea of colour and scent, Faga's front garden. Among the lush exuberant mix of flowers are taro and bananas – Maopo's contribution.

'Twelve, okay?' Sam calls to him. He nods.

Opening the front door with his key, he goes into the corridor which is alive with the smell of coconut oil, the smell of his growing up. Coconut oil is Faga's cure for everything. His sisters and cousins hate it because they don't want to be identified as Coconuts. Yeah, but he loves it, is proud of it, flaunts it. 'Faga!' he calls.

'Is that you?' Her voice comes from the kitchen. He finds her crouched on the floor, cleaning the cupboard under the sink. He wants to help her. But he doesn't, because Faga doesn't like being considered old and helpless. He waits until she's standing up, her thin frail body trembling from the strain of rising from the floor. 'Can you see my eyes anywhere?' she asks in Samoan. He finds her glasses on the bench and gives them to her. 'You go in and sit with Maopo, while I prepare some lunch.' He hesitates. 'Go on. I've cooked some chop suey and taro. You look too skinny, Iona. Too much palagi food.' Her mind and memory are still strong, but she's slowing down, becoming forgetful, sometimes confusing the past and the present.

Maopo is in the middle of the bed, still, vacant eyes staring into the ceiling. Bed-ridden, unable to recognise anyone else but Faga. Maopo's emaciated face, with the eyes deeply buried in their hollow sockets, reminds him of the face of an owl. Been like this for about a year. And worsening. Iona hesitates at the door. Can't take this any more, watching his grandad being eaten up by old age. First his sight, then his hearing, his body, then control of his bodily functions, cruel fucking humiliation for someone who'd lived so comfortably in and with his body and senses. Grace, marvellous coordination of movement and muscle… And you can't do a thing to stop the final humiliation, this slow death.

He sits down in the chair by the bed. Smoothes down the sheet on his grandad's chest. 'Ya remember that time, Maopo, when we were still at Freeman's Bay, in that flea-ridden house we loved because it was home, that time you came home drunk and, instead of being angry, Faga asked you to sing your favourite song and you sang in your fresh-off-the-boat English:

"Pa, Pa, Plackie Siki

Have youse any valu?

One for le master and one for le teine

Who lives down de way…"'

Iona laughs and says, 'Ya remember that, Maopo? I learned right then how to speak FOB English, like you.'

During most of his visits, he fills the silences with Maopo with reminiscences from their life together, stories that weave into other stories, telling them the way Maopo used to.

Now, as he's doing that, anger starts intruding. Why the fuck did you ever come to this country, this land of the albinos, which continues to treat you as nobodies, dumb powerless Coconuts, FOB, to be used in the factories and shit jobs they won't touch? He stops. It's unfair. That's not how his grandparents had seen it. New Zealand had offered them a chance to be out of the poverty of Samoa, to have work, get their kids a good education. 'Yeah, I learned early from you and Faga, Maopo. Remember, how I used to help Faga go round the streets on rubbish collection days, collecting all the cans and bottles from the rubbish bins? Remember? Sometimes Faga was blue with the cold. And the humiliation. I knew why she and you were doing that: it was to keep us alive. But I promised myself, no bastard – brown or albino or black or yellow or purple – was ever going to do that to me or my sisters or to you when I was able to support you.' He pauses, and caresses Maopo's hand. 'I decided then, you and Faga weren't going to need for anything.' Pauses. 'You learned early never to ask me and my cousins where we got the money, food, and other stuff we started bringing home.' Chuckles. 'You didn't know, but at the age of twelve, me and Ofu and Sam controlled the paper runs in central Freeman's Bay. Yeah, any kid who wanted to deliver newspapers had to pay us 15 percent!'

During lunch with Faga he does nearly all the talking. As usual, she expects him to tell her, in great detail, what he and the rest of their aiga have been doing that week. 'It's good, Iona, that you keep an eye on everyone, it's your duty because you're the most Samoan. Maopo raised you to be the head of our aiga,' she keeps interrupting him. 'You got into lots of trouble, eh, boy?' She chortles. 'Yes, right from your first week at Freeman's Bay Primary.' She continues laughing.

Their Samoan names got them into trouble first. Iona, Malia, Ofu, Samuelu, Pelu and Upega. Their teachers and the palagi students couldn't be bothered pronouncing their Samoan names properly, so they named them Jonah, Mary, Melanie, Sam, Joe and Nick.

When she was first called Mary by her teachers, Malia started whimpering softly, and all that day refused to obey her teacher. Ofu stamped her feet repeatedly when the other kids teased her about her new name, Melanie; she scratched one boy across his neck and the teacher ordered her out to stand in the centre of the playground. Samuelu, who didn't say much, ever, grunted his disapproval at being called Sam, and, when his teacher turned to write on the blackboard, gave him the up-you sign, much to the other kids' delight. On being renamed Joe and Nick, Pelu and Upega folded their arms across their defiant chests and refused to budge from their seats until lunchtime. However, all of them within a few weeks relented and got stuck with their palagi names for the rest of their lives. But *he* refused to give in. He slugged the first boy who called him Jonah.

Now as he relives that, he enjoys, yes, *enjoys* the sharp, defiant crunch of his punch. The teacher strapped him. Not a whimper or tear. Next morning when Miss Balsham called him Jonah, he looked defiantly into her fat face, and said, 'Miss, my name is Iona, I-O-NA!' The headmaster reprimanded him for that. A few days later Miss Balsham's car, which was parked in front of the Ponsonby Picture Theatre, got four slashed tyres and a smashed rear window. Even now, years and years later, he enjoys remembering how, after that, she and the other teachers pronounced his name correctly.

'You and Grandad always stood by us, Faga. Always.'

'Yes, but we got fed up with you at times. We were afraid of the police and the courts. We're ignorant people, Iona. We couldn't speak English … At times, Maopo was sick with fear when he had to come to court and face those awful police and judges …'

'But you always stood by me, Faga.'

'That's what aiga is, Iona. You know that!' Wicked smile. 'And you've always been a quick learner, eh, Iona? You learned from your first time in the Boys' Home and Mt Eden, how not to find yourself in there again, eh?' They laugh together. 'And you make sure your sisters never got into trouble with the police.'

Faga pauses again, then, turning her thick spectacles on him, asks slowly, 'Are you ever afraid of anything, Iona?'

'Lots of things, Faga …'

'You know what I mean, Iona. We've always been afraid that you have no fear. Not even of God!'

'That's not true,' he tries to say. He knows what she's going to say next – she says it every visit.

'You must never stop believing in God. We've survived well in this country because of our church and the Almighty. Never forget that, Iona.'

Jut before twelve, after he's washed, dried and put the dishes away, he goes in to his grandfather, kisses him on the forehead, smoothes back his hair, and retreats into the sitting room where he stands at the front window, watching the street for his car to return. Remembering, he takes $200 out of his wallet and puts it under the tanoa on the mantelpiece – his weekly contribution to his grandparents' upkeep.

His car noses darkly up the street and stops at the front gate. Fucking shit, he can't believe it when Sam and Nick get out wearing black Raybans, black suits, black polonecks, black boots and number one haircuts. Talk about attracting unwanted attention to themselves!

'Faga!' he calls. No reply. 'Faga, I'm going!' He starts for the front door. 'Ou ke koe sau fo'i i le vaiaso lea! Fa!'

He shuts the front door just as Sam and Nick hit the front steps. They start greeting him. He brushes past, between them. Gets into the back seat, slams the car door, sits staring ahead in menacing silence. Sam and Nick get in meekly. Absolutely brainless, like most young Hamos in the city: arrogant, brash, dumb showoffs!

'How's Faga and Maopo?' Sam asks. Iona refuses to answer, or let them off the hook.

Through the lunchtime streets of Otahuhu, Onehunga and then along the motorway, along the Manukau. The strong smell of hot sun and low tide, wind weaving in from the south.

Sam turns in to the Pacific Tavern and drives round to the carpark behind. 'We've arranged the meeting,' Nick informs him. Iona gets out. 'Rangi and Dodo are waiting in the back bar.'

Sam and Nick start following him. He stops unexpectedly and, without turning to look at them, says, 'Go home and get out of those … those fucking costumes!' He waits.

'Okay, Iona,' Sam apologises.

'Ya look like faafafiges with ice-blocks shoved up ya ufa!'

'Sorry, Iona!' Nick tries.

'You've learned nothing! What's the rule? Go on, I wanna hear it!'

'Be invisible,' Sam begins.

'Blend in with the people,' Nick continues.

'Be back in twenty minutes,' Iona orders, and hurries to the front entrance of the tavern. Cousins, my cousins, who owe me their lives. Ever since Freeman's Bay, he's had to save them from their stupidities and flaws. All he asks for is loyalty.

He first met Rangi and Dodo in the Boys' Home, and they continued their friendship, a few years later, in Paremoremo Prison, where he'd been for a year. His friends now live in Kaitaia and are part of his larger aiga and business, coming to Auckland every few months, where they meet at different pre-arranged bars. Iona likes the back bar at the Pacific Tavern, with its mainly Polynesian clientele and its expansive windows that open out to the park to let in a steady stream of fresh air. No smoking allowed there, either. He hates smoking. Kills ya! Fucks up your lungs and brains.

The bar is filling up. Many greet him. Some wave respectfully. He recognises many of the Samoans: some are members of his family's church. They part and let him through to Rangi and Dodo at the table under the back windows.

'Hi, Iona, welcome!' Barry Winston, the palagi owner who's

serving behind the bar, calls to him. Iona waves back, perfunctorily. *Mister* Barry Winston's a grateful, satisfied client. No trouble ever at his tavern. No, sir. No fights or burglaries or staff strikes or scams or whatever. I make sure of that. At a price. At a good and fair price.

'Kia ora, Bro!' Rangi greets him. They hongi and embrace. He hongis Dodo. Great to see them, bloody staunch. 'A drink, Bro?' Rangi asks. He tells him he just wants a Diet Coke. Dodo goes off to the bar.

'Good ta see ya again, Rangi. How's Jeanne and the kids?'

'Good, good.' Trim, fit, a compact unit of boundless energy, determination and no bullshit, Rangi is loyal once he knows you're straight and generous with him. Good also to have him in your aiga because of his skills with his fists and a baseball bat.

'How's business?' Rangi asks.

'Strong and improving at a growth rate of 3 to 4 percent!' Iona mimics Winston Peters. They laugh. Dodo arrives with their drinks.

'Kia ora, e hoa!' Dodo salutes.

'Manuia!' he replies. They drink. More customers are arriving, but they keep away from their table. They merely wave, call out their greetings, and go elsewhere.

'Everything's been arranged for your stay,' Iona tells his friends. 'Sam and Nick'll look after ya. Anything you need, ask them.'

'Thanks. I'm sure we're goin' to have a great time!' Rangi replies.

'As usual!' laughs Dodo, the dark tattoos on his arms dancing.

'Sam tells me the stuff's the best grade?' Iona remarks.

'Fantastic crop,' Dodo says. 'And a lot of it.'

'As you instructed, we're holding back half the crop so the prices stay up, Iona,' Rangi explains. Iona pokes him playfully on the shoulder. 'Ah'm learning, eh, Bro. Learning about supply and demand and stuff like that.'

While they're laughing, Iona surprises them. 'Usual price?' he asks. Rangi and Dodo glance at each other. Not usual to discuss prices so early and so openly, but then Iona does unexpected things that always result in bigger profits for everyone. 'How about 5 percent on last May's prices?' Rangi nods and they shake hands. 'To be paid through the usual channels?' Iona asks.

Through the crowded room saunter Sam and Nick, dressed in jeans and sports shoes, bald heads covered with blue balaclavas, like the people, not sticking out like peacocks for the cops to de-cock. The people part respectfully and let them through.

Iona refuses to look at his cousins as they hongi Rangi and Dodo, who offer them drinks. They glance at Iona and politely refuse the offer of drinks: no alcohol while Iona does business.

Swiftly Iona reaches up and whips off their balaclavas, for all the others to marvel and laugh at his cousins' shiny bald heads. 'Da da!' he introduces them.

'Fuck, man!' Rangi whistles. Barney Winston and Iona's Samoan elders lead the laughter and applause and whistling.

'Bow, ya mongrels!' he orders his cousins, who hesitate and then bow. 'Lower!' Iona emphasises. They do.

Quickly, he instructs Sam and Nick about looking after their 'northern brothers' and the crop. He embraces Rangi and Dodo. 'Give my love to the missus and the kids, Bro! See ya!' He turns; he can feel everyone watching him as he paces through the crowd. They wave and call their farewells; he smiles and keeps waving his arm high in the air.

Yes, he likes that: respect, fa'aloalo, his grandad calls it. He's earned their respect – and admiration. And they come to him for help when they need it.

Above all else, his grandad before he lost his mind had said, 'Iona, our aiga and community respect and love you for the generous way you always help them.'

On his way through thick traffic to K Road he rings Ofu, his sister, on his cellphone. He's the only person who gets away with calling her Ofu. Everyone else has called her Melanie since she insisted at the age of twelve that that was her preferred name. He gets away with it because he had paid for most of her university education, got her into Buffin, Mutle and Blake, the law firm he uses. He continues to be her biggest client. He is also head of their aiga, and her fearless protector.

'Talofa, Ofu!' he greets her. 'Why are ya ashamed of your Hamo name?' he jokes. Deep hurt pause at the other end. He laughs. 'Jus' been to see Faga and Grandad. Faga tells me you've not been to see them since Loku-a-Kamaiki. That's no good, Sis. That's not family.'

'I've been very busy, Brother,' she tries to placate him.

'With that palagi boyfriend? Boyfriends come and go. Faga and Maopo are *our* parents,' Iona whispers. 'And they're old and unwell!'

'And without them I wouldn't be alive and well today, right?' she mimics him.

'Right, Sis! Right! And you'd better not forget it.' He's into his Marlon-Brando-as-Don-Corleone act.

'I'll go and see them tonight,' she pronounces, and before he reminds her, adds, 'And I'll take Faga her favourite chocolate…'

'Don't forget your cash contribution to their welfare, too, Sis.'

Quickly, he details the deal with Rangi and Dodo and the price and the amount to be 'transferred'. She updates him on three property transactions he's involved in. 'They're not shifting on prices,' she tells him.

'Give it another two weeks. With a little *persuasion* they'll come down.' Chuckles.

It's slow along K Road. Chocka with traffic. Ahh. He U-turns swiftly into the vacant carpark on the other side. Always lucky in women, business and carparks! his second sister, Malia, keeps telling him. A lot of truth in that, he thinks.

Slots a fifty-cent coin into the parking meter.

When he was a boy, K Road was full of Pacific Islanders, Maori and working-class people. He'd loved shopping there with his grandparents. Since the middle-class yuppie wankers, mainly palagi, started moving into the inner city, most of *his* people were gone into the suburbs, into South Auckland.

He recognises some of the drunks and ex-whores on the benches. He looks up. Ahead, right in his gaze, two young Samoan fa'afafine in sleek black, immaculate makeup and high heels, are sashaying musically towards him. 'Hi, Iona!' they greet him, in unison. He bows and waves. They sashay past, dizzying smell of Opium.

Trade Aid Shop. Love shopping here. He enters. Not too many customers. Among them, a couple of Samoans. They nod; he nods and smiles. The two shop assistants are young women without makeup: plain, appropriate representatives for the products from the Third and Fourth Worlds. One of them, Jill, talks to him when he's there.

Gotta support the poor and exploited, he muses. Samoa's still in that category. As a boy, when he came home howling because a teacher had called him Sambo, Faga sat him down and said, 'Iona, there's racism and injustice in this wicked world. You can't change that all by yourself. Nor should you try. Most importantly, work with it. Having racism right in your face shouldn't stop you from doing what you have to do.'

Yeah, he thinks as he examines a book by Reynold Thunder,

powerful countries, usually white, fucked the poor countries, usually black or brown or yellow, sucked the juices out of them. It's all gotta do with power, and who has it, who fucks who, who licks whose arse and other sensitive vital parts, to get what they want. It's all business, nothing personal, except when they try and fuck you and those you love and respect.

'Anything we can do for you?' Jill asks. He always buys something, several things.

'Thank you, I'm jus' looking.' As he wanders on, something, a blur, tugs at the corner of his vision. He stops, looks to his left, up to the top shelf. The Owl. He looks again. About a foot high and half hidden by a framed photograph. Reaches up, pushes the picture aside. There, swallowing him up, with Its huge blue-black, shimmering eyes. Of ebony wood and polished to a marble sheen. Simple symmetry, almost all face and eyes and beak and talons. Hefty and squat. He touches Its shoulder, suspiciously. Nothing. Runs his forefinger down Its left wing, all the time he's caught in the Bird's all-encompassing gaze. Fathomless, shimmering depths in which his reflection shifts and swims.

Gingerly, he clasps the Bird, with both hands around Its talons and base, and holding It in front of him at a safe distance, he takes It and places It on the glass counter in front of Jill. 'It's beautiful, eh?' she remarks. 'It came in our last shipment.' He nods, once. It's fierce, yeah, *manaful*. As the light plays over It, It bristles and watches you. 'It's $120,' she says. He unfolds his wallet and pulls out the notes.

Jill starts wrapping It up in tissue paper. He is suddenly in the depths of a tropical rainforest. Blue, dank, humid light. In Samoa? I've been there before. Upolu? In my childhood before New Zealand, who with? My grandad? Yes, with Maopo.

Then into his hearing slides the deep resonant hooting, and the slow-flapping of wings, the determined take-off, the branch shuddering as the Bird leaps into the forest stillness, the long slow weaving through the canopy, body and feathers sleek with sun and shadow, as It searches and stalks the undergrowth below …

'You've given me too much,' Jill rescues him. He tries to smile. Returns the notes to his wallet.

He is safe; the Bird is wrapped in delicate tissue paper and contained in the Trade Aid shopping bag. 'Thank you again!' Jill says. He notices that her eyes are an unusual translucent blue.

'I collect owls,' he says and immediately feels stupid for saying it – bragging? Showing off?

He turns, bag handles grasped firmly in his left hand, and hurries out, the weight of the Bird anchoring him.

As he rejoins the current of shoppers on the street, he again questions his inexplicable attraction – or is it addiction? – to things beyond order and safety, to creatures and happenings at the edge and over-the-edge, beyond reason, logic, the law, the usual, the accepted. Like re-exploring the wild possibilities of sex for the first time with a new lover, like driving beyond the speed limit risking a violent death, like smashing the bastards who're trying to intimidate you, yeah, especially that, and enjoying it, like diving into Grandad's wild gaze as he raves about the ancient atua of Samoa, the pagan atua, the fearless atua, before the fucking missionaries outlawed them, yeah, like…

The Red Hibiscus Café and Bar is owned by Sheena and Dave Blonsky. Palagi but aiga. Dave and his sister, Milly, and their crazy dad and alcoholic mother had lived next door to them in Wellington Street. Dave and Milly tried to escape their violent parents and poverty by spending nearly all their time in Iona's home, and Faga and Maopo had treated them as their own. When Social Welfare took the kids away from Mr and Mrs Blonsky and put them in foster homes, Dave kept returning to Iona's.

He had helped Dave and Sheena set up the café, but he'd

refused a shareholding. Only two free meals a week, he'd suggested, as payment. Sheena and another waitress are serving at the bar. Now he lunches there twice a week.

Today, the place is full and noisy. Sheena waves and points to the back of the restaurant. NO SMOKING ALLOWED. 'See ya in a minute, Iona!' she calls.

Nearly all palagi customers. Again, he feels self-conscious as he strolls to the back and waits for his table. Kim, the university music student waitress who usually serves him, is suddenly beside him. 'Bloody crowded, eh?' he sighs.

'Yeah, but there's always room for you,' Kim replies, respectfully. He follows her.

Attractive in black body tights and cotton blouse, she moves like an athlete. Tight arse and flanks, thighs, back. But no – hands off. She's staff – and he never fucks staff. Bad for business relationships and morale.

Sheena embraces and kisses him on the cheek. 'Shit, Iona, you're looking fitter than all of us put together!'

'Yeah, comes from having to work hard to feed, house and clothe a large, hungry aiga.' He waits while Sheena and Kim unfold the table under the large oil painting of a red hibiscus, place two chairs at it, and Kim wipes and sets it.

221

Sheena came into his aiga six years before, when she married Dave (with Iona's consent). She's a descendant of a German-Samoan family who'd migrated to Auckland in the 1940s. You can say she is Samoan, of a kind.

'We can barely cope with the number today,' she says.

'But you're making lots of bread, eh!' he laughs.

'Some bloody consolation,' she says. 'Shall I take that?' She refers to his parcel.

Shaking his head, he says, 'No. It's going to sit with me.' He places the parcel on the opposite side of the table.

'What is it?'

'An atua,' he admits, finally. She looks puzzled; he doesn't care. Mysteries, that's what keeps the blood kicking and searching.

'A god from the Trade Aid Shop?'

'Yeah, from the Trade Aid Shop,' he laughs.

'I'm sure Dave'll understand that more, so I'll tell him you're here. I've got to serve.' She rushes off.

Through the partition that separates the kitchen, he can see Dave and another chef sweating as they cook at the stoves.

'The usual?' Kim asks.

He shakes his head. 'Just a salad and coffee today. You're a very bright university student, do you know what owls eat?'

She is surprised, but doesn't joke when she sees that he is serious. 'They're birds of prey, eh?' He nods again. 'Well, I suppose they eat live rats and things like that.' She pauses, impish smile. 'And, Iona, we ain't got any of those!'

He starts chortling, softly. 'Kim, you keep surprising me. Yeah, what other surprises have you got in store for me?' He regrets the invitation and is relieved when she smiles, invitingly, and then says, 'I'd lose my job. Dave and Sheena have instructed us to treat you as off limits.'

She hurries off to get his meal.

He sits contemplating the Bird in the parcel.

Kim and Dave return with his meal – green salad with bacon and avocado, and coffee. Dave embraces him. 'It's Faga's birthday next Tuesday, isn't it?' he reminds Iona. Dave always remembers and does the right thing, reciprocates the people who love and help him.

'Shit, Dave, I'd forgotten about it.'

'I'll bake her favourite cake…'

'Which is?' Iona tests him.

Dave pretends he's trying to remember, then chuckling, declares, 'Carrot cake. Gotcha, Bro. And I'll get some fresh oysters and mussels …'

'… and crayfish …'

'From the Sea Mart, cook it the way she loves it …' Dave stops. Ponders. 'She's not well, is she, Iona?' Iona shakes his head. 'It's unfair, isn't it, Bro?' Dave adds.

'How's my nieces?' Iona changes the subject.

For the next fifteen minutes they talk about their relatives and aiga and friends. Sheena joins them, and details what's been happening to them that week. Iona finishes eating and, sipping his coffee, watches her and how Dave is again at the edge while she *directs* their life. He wishes, again, that she was *less* palagi. He knows she's leading the conversation to business and he's annoyed about it because you never discuss business over a meal. But that isn't going to stop her from getting there because he knows from the past that Dave, though angry about it, isn't going to stop her either. '… And if ya talk to the other business people on K Road, Iona, they'll tell you, angrily, that all the rents are going up again. Blood-sucking bastards!' She pauses. 'Did ya know, Iona, that only last Friday the bastard who represents the company that owns this complex came and told us our rent is going up by 6 percent, at the end of the month.' She stops and looks at Iona, who's trying not to look at Dave, who is looking up at the red hibiscus painting. 'Bloody crooks!'

He sighs and says, emphatically, 'Sis, jus' ring Melanie and tell her I told you to ring her about it.'

'Thanks, Iona,' Sheena says. She doesn't even bother to give it time; she leaves to help the other waiters.

'Sorry about that, Iona,' Dave apologises.

Iona smiles, 'She was late coming into our aiga, so she's never quite understood how *we* do things. But, as you know, our aiga and I have a lot of alofa for her. Yeah, Dave, because she's your wife and the mother of my nieces. I also know you don't like telling her off.' Pauses. 'I don't like correcting adults either, Bro.'

Kim comes and starts clearing the table. Iona asks her for an orange juice.

'So when are ya going to ask me?' Iona asks Dave.

'About what?' Dave continues pretending.

'Fuck, mate, about *that*.' He reaches over and pats the head of the parcel.

'Okay, okay, what's it?'

'Open it, Bro. Open it!'

No one in the lobby of his apartment building. He takes the lift up to the top floor. No one in the corridor as he strolls to his apartment through the white summer light streaming in from the row of windows on his right. For a moment he thinks his body is turning into white vapour. Apart from Ron Buckle, who built the apartments and sold them, no one knew he had that apartment. They believed his home to be his house in O'Neil Street, Ponsonby.

The apartment took up half of the top storey, with a spacious sitting room, three bedrooms, two bathrooms and a balcony a quarter the size of a tennis court. Through various sources he'd heard that Ron Buckle, after pre-selling the apartments, had gambled away much of that money, and was desperate for finance to finish the building. It didn't take long, through Buffin, Mutle and Blake, for him to arrange that money – at the interest rate of a 'free' apartment, this apartment, his secret nest.

He puts the parcel on the coffee table, hurries to his bedroom, changes into an ie lavalava, returns and sits by the parcel.

The sitting room is sparsely furnished: sofa, two soft chairs – all in white; on the far wall a corny photograph of his village and church; a line of family photos on the mantelpieces. Nothing else. Monastic, he likes to think of it. Like his grandfather, he has reduced his life, in this apartment, to the bare essentials. Real power and happiness lie beyond material things. It's in you, in your ability, sight, belief in yourself. That's all you need to cope even with fear, and with any threat from your enemies. Yes, he has control of his life.

Lovingly, he unpacks the Bird, uses a piece of flannel to wipe It until It is glistening like the profound blackness of the retina of an eye. Then, cradling It in his right arm like a child, he carries It out to the balcony and the boundless world of summer light.

He stands at the railing. Above him the heavens stretch up and up in a mix of white cloud and haze and blazing sun. Below him, tumbling away into the harbour and the bridge and Rangitoto and the Gulf, the city. His city. His hunting ground.

With both hands, gripping the Bird's talons, he raises It, slowly, inevitably, above his head for all the city and bays and sky to salute, in awe. Awesome.

All around, the air starts trembling with the heart-like beat of the Bird's hooting and slow flapping of wings…

From *The Best of Albert Wendt's Short Stories.*

Autumn and Waiheke

STEVE BRAUNIAS

This is nice. The softer light, the cooler air, the sky that settles in for an early night: April is the tenderest month. It's true that Auckland doesn't do autumn very well. You really want the South Island, or riverside towns like Cambridge and Taihape, for the brittle colours, the fragile collapses. You want the smell of coal in Greymouth at dusk, the white sea at early morning in Mt Maunganui.

You want all the sadness of autumn. I love it. Age, and death, and love, and memory – it's like twilight all the time. A friend of mine hates twilight: it makes him depressed, anxious, powerless: you bet he loathes and detests autumn.

He needs a lot of company this time of year. Mostly I just laugh at his fears, pour him another drink, and sit by as he blathers away in a desperate attempt to combat the implacable silence of autumn. I'm not sure, but I think I know how he feels – a sense the next few months are like a trial separation, that life becomes an outline of something seen in the distance. Remote months, months like the end of an affair. 'Kill him so that he can feel he is dying,' as Caligula instructed.

Bring it on. You could say I was dying to see the dying of the summer light last weekend, when daylight saving closed its account, and autumn could officially get down to its melancholy business. I decided to leave town. All I might notice of the changing seasons in Auckland would be a bunch of style bores dressed in black on Saturday night, and black on Sunday night.

Where to go? My wife wanted to consult a map. All we had was a world atlas. Uruguay showed promise, and they say the Seychelles are pleasant this time of year. I rattled off a few rather more convenient destinations: Thames, Waihi, Helensville. Clearly, I was overexcited.

We ended up sailing on Saturday afternoon to Waiheke Island, where Jenny had arranged bed and breakfast at Appletree Cottage. Our hostess was Betty. She had lived on the island for 60 years, she said, and everyone knew her. I looked at the list of things to do. 'Sift compost. Chop firewood. Open oysters.' Could I help with anything? No, said Betty, she had a squadron of blokes on call: 'You just enjoy yourself, dear.'

Good idea. We had a lovely weekend. After dinner on

Saturday night, we mooched along the beach, striped with the long shadows of dusk. It was summer's last shout – the kind of evening you never expect to grow old. I stuck a toetoe branch down the back of my neck. We found a green bug in much distress, upside down on the sand, and carried it inside a shell to the grass. Out in the water, a woman wearing a blue bikini jumped off the stern of a launch. There was a sickle moon.

Because the clocks were turned back an hour during the night, we got extra value for money at Appletree Cottage. Breakfast was leisurely. In the TV lounge, Betty listened to a choir on *Praise Be*. 'We will cling to the old rugged cross.' Then she talked about her garden, which was greatly enriched by elephant dung – she knew a man who owned a circus. She also talked about a man who tried to live in the watchhouse of a boat that had gone to ground on Blackpool beach, but 'he was taken away'.

Betty made and sold crafts. There were pussycat cushion covers (her own cat, Pamela, would turn 15 on Tuesday), and signs warning against piddling on the toilet seat. But by now the sky had opened wide, and was thoroughly blue.

Tremendous. We swam, we hoofed around to three different beaches, we wolfed down some bananas; perched on a rock, I read Boswell's *Life of Johnson*, while Jenny lay on the sand and filled her pretty head with Stephen Jay Gould.

Idyllic, casual, downright happy – where was melancholic autumn? It had to wait, arriving, inevitably, at dusk, which now began to fall, slowly and tenderly, collapsing the bright day, from about six that night.

We caught the boat back at 6.45 pm. And that was how I saw the first dying of the light of autumn – at sea, the water turning black, the sky revealing a mess of stars. There was a chill in the air. Summer had flown the coop. It felt like something new was about to happen.

From *Fool's Paradise*.

An eyeland adventure with old winds

SISTAR S'PACIFIC

My homeland
Auckland
Tamaki-ma-kau-rau

Dead volcanoes draped in sparse
finery and forgotten winds litter this land

There are dragons on the streets,
spewing up flowers and coconuts

Handsome moths and flying foxes are
throwing fab parties with all you can eat

Full tuskers getting lei'd, with garlands of birds
singing songs filled with thunder and lightning

Great octopusi dressed in satin, dancing with whales
that talk to great stones that fall from the sky

Whai'ding my way home, on the back of a flounder
with a diamond back and centipede edges

Off to bathe in black sands
with a heavy moon at my side

The harbour is in soft ripple and
in up and coming phantasm

Rangitoto is peaking to right in my eye... and I
see the sun descend between lush, bushy mountains

Where once fairies roamed in a great rain forest
that spread coast to coast

Above, a great shark is revealed in the sky inside
a bright, light night, feeling still and well tendered

Old winds are whispering of Kupe's passing, fresh from Hawaiki
chasing red ripples that later shed blood

Oh 'City of sails' can you hear them, I pray they not be forgotten
for they will lead me home to Hawaiki.

ACKNOWLEDGEMENTS

Thanks are due to authors, copyright holders and publishers for their permission to reproduce copyright material in this book.

Denis Baker, *On a Distant Island* (David Ling Publishing 2002); James K Baxter, *Ode to Auckland* – extract (Oxford University Press 1979), with the permission of the copyright owner J.C. Baxter; Steve Braunias, 'Autumn' from *Fool's Paradise* (Random House 2001); Diane Brown, *if the tongue fits* (Tandem Press 1999); Glenn Colquhoun, 'Bred in South Auckland' from *The Art of Walking Upright* (Steele Roberts 1999); Allen Curnow, 'Lone Kauri Road' (1972), reproduced by permission of the copyright owner Jeny Curnow, c/- Tim Curnow, Literary Agent, Sydney; Janet Frame, *An Angel at My Table* (Hutchinson 1984); Maurice Gee, *Going West* (Faber & Faber 1992); Charlotte Grimshaw, *Provocation* (Little Brown 1999) and *Guilt* (Little Brown 2000), reproduced by permission of PFD, the author's agents; Witi Ihimaera, *Nights in the Gardens of Spain* (Reed Publishing 1995); Kevin Ireland, 'Pity about the Gulls' from *Selected Poems* (Hazard Press 1997); Anna Jackson, 'Coffee and Cheese with Gudrun and Ursula' from *The Long Road to Tea-Time* (Auckland University Press 2000) and 'Who is Reading Poetry in 2021' (Artspace 2002); Stephanie Johnson, *Belief* (Random House 2000); Bruce Mason, *The End of the Golden Weather* (Nelson Price Milburn 1962), with the permission of Victoria University Press; Paula Morris, *Queen of Beauty* (Penguin 2002); Bob Orr, 'Container Terminal' from *Breeze* (Auckland University Press 1991); Merimeri Penfold, 'Tamaki of a Hundred Lovers'; John Pule, *Burn My Head in Heaven* (Penguin 1998); Sarah Quigley,

After Robert (Penguin 1999); Rosanna Raymond (Sistar S'pacific), 'An Eyeland Adventure with Old Winds' (Artspace 2002); Frank Sargeson, *Memoirs of a Peon* (MacGibbon and Kee 1965), with the permission of the Frank Sargeson Trust; Maurice Shadbolt, *Dove on the Waters* (David Ling Publishing 1996); Tina Shaw, *City of Reeds* (Penguin 2000); C.K. Stead, *Talking About O'Dwyer* (Penguin 1999), and Sonnet 3 of 'Twenty-two Sonnets' from *Poems of a Decade* (Pilgrims South Press 1983); Robert Sullivan, 'Onehunga Bay' and 'Message from Mangere' from *Jazz Waiata* (Auckland University Press 1990); Peter Wells, *Long Loop Home: A Memoir* (Random House 2001); Albert Wendt, 'The Don'ts of Whistling' (extract) and 'The Bird' from *The Best of Albert Wendt's Short Stories* (Random House 1999).